Second Chances

A Contemporary Romance Novel

Lucy Appadoo

This book is dedicated to those who have struggled with bullying at school. May you be free of the past.

Contents

Chapter 1

ANGIE'S DELUXE BOOKSHOP

Angelina Regio reached up to stack books on the tall deep-blue bookshelf, her arm aching after sorting out new stock. She massaged her bicep and winced at the aches and pains. In any new venture, Angie liked to go all in rather than ease into things. Her friends always chastised her for pushing herself too hard, and the aching joints and pains were the result.

Her eyes roamed her newly established bookshop, which took a lot of grit and effort to make spotless. The blue carpeted flooring gave off a fresh scent, and the smell of new books made her heart soar. Decorative Australian flags and bright globe lights hung down from the ceiling and gave the bookshop a warm and inviting ambience.

Angelina, whose friends called her Angie, stepped behind the counter and leaned into a cardboard box containing new books. Flicking a burgundy, brown fringe out of her eye, she grasped a book and put it on another bookshelf. Her long hair cascaded loosely down over her shoulders, and she regretted not tying it up. It was a hindrance, always catching in the pages of books. Beads of sweat lined the back of her neck, and she was short of breath after a two-hour stint of physical exertion that morning.

She faced her business partner and best friend, Maddy, heading into the back part of the shop holding bags of food and two bottles of water.

"Hey, Angie. I bring food."

The bottles almost toppled over, but Angie reached forward and caught them. She smiled at her friend, whose short, light brown waves bobbed as she settled the food onto the counter. Maddy wasn't much taller than the front counter, but Angie would kill for her slim figure and hazel eyes, which sometimes pierced into her own when Maddy worried about the slightest things.

"Thanks, Maddy. I'm starving."

Angie pulled out a warm cheese and ham croissant, sinking her teeth into the soft, flaky texture, butter dripping down her chin. Wiping her mouth with a napkin, she stood by the counter with Maddy opposite. "It's been six months, Maddy. We need more customers just to meet costs. We have to make this bookshop work. The online bookstores are killing our business."

Maddy nodded while holding onto her hash brown. "It takes time, Angie. Let me worry about the numbers. I do the books, after all."

"But we should have more steady sales by now." She chewed more of the croissant, savouring the delicious flavours.

Maddy grinned. "I know, but you're a people person. You'll find ways to attract more customers." She sighed. "The bookshop will be booming soon. You'll see. Cutting out the voluntary work at the hospital will pay off. You'll be needed here on Saturdays." She spoke through a mouth full of food.

Angie knit her brows. "You're right. I'll think of something. I hope. This is our new baby."

Angie had known Maddy since primary school, and they'd been best friends ever since. She'd had Angie's back through the dark times, and there wasn't anyone else Angie would rather be in this bookshop business with than Maddy. Growing bored at their nine-to-five jobs, they had planned to open the bookshop together. After a few years working as a marketing executive, Angie managed to save enough for her half of the investment. Maddy had come up with the other half working as a financial analyst. Now, their collective love of books and business was all around them. From the smell of paper and ink to the creaking of the wood floors, Angie felt at home in their little bookshop. She prayed with all her soul that they wouldn't need to close their doors. If business didn't pick up soon, though, they would be doing exactly that. All their dreams and plans would be for nothing.

With Maddy's accounting skills and Angelina's business savvy mind, they could surely make this new enterprise work. Angie and Maddy had done well for their twenty-seven years.

The bookshop had a staircase out the back, which led to large bay windows and walking space. The previous owner had used part of that space as a small gallery to display paintings. Next door was a vacant building that her stepfather, Jack, had purchased for her in hopes that she would eventually expand the business. Expanding the store seemed out of the question with the first six months of poor sales.

Angie finished drinking her water then threw all the breakfast scraps into the nearby bin. Together, they opened the roller door and welcomed the three waiting customers standing outside. Maddy made her way into the store while Angie put out a small whiteboard sign to promote selected books. She needed to find the customers who would buy at full price but target bargain-hunters too. The promotions wouldn't be a regular occurrence but a way to bring in new customers to build the business.

Maddy served the first customer of the day and smiled as the man rattled on about the ills of the world while shaking his head. Poor Maddy, having to deal with someone who complained about everything.

Angie changed focus and peered at the entrance. She needed paying customers, and it didn't look like any of the morning visitors were buying. She was walking to the counter when in the corner of her eye, she caught a familiar face. She flinched and her stomach seemed to sink right out of her. What was *he* doing here?

Enrico looked a little older but hadn't changed much with his short, black glossy hair, striking bright blue eyes, a strong jawline, and shaped eyebrows. His attractiveness was never in question, but behind that chiselled physique hid a viper—a bully who thought he was God's gift to women. Angie doubted ten years could change someone that much. Once a bully, always a bully.

Angie scanned the room for Maddy and found her still busy with the customer. Enrico turned in her direction but didn't look surprised to see her. With a hesitant step, he approached her and lowered his gaze. "Hello, Angie."

Her bottom lip trembled, and her arms fell loosely to the sides. "Enrico. What are you doing here?" Angie took a deep breath and fought off the images of her past, which still troubled her.

Enrico cleared his throat, hesitating. "I need a book about wood carving. Would you have something?" He averted his eyes and stared out into the distance.

She nodded, wishing she didn't have to be the ever professional and could tell him to get lost. "Over here." Angie slid her fingers across the middle row of a range of handyman and craft books and pulled one out. She promptly deposited it into his hand. "Here. There are a few others on this shelf. Feel free to browse."

Angie's throat was dry, and her legs unsteady. She made her way back to the counter without looking back, trying to calm her nerves. Quickly, she assisted another customer while gazing briefly at Enrico, who flicked through the book and intermittently eyed her with curiosity. Why was the bastard here? Had he come to push the knife deeper into her chest? He acted as if he'd done nothing to her all those years ago. The nerve of him coming into her place of business.

He eventually made his way to the counter. She quickly entered his purchases, the wood carving book she had given him and a thriller novel. She grabbed his credit card, their fingers brushing. She ignored the tingle and the way his eyes scanned her face as she handed him his receipt. "Enjoy the books."

Enrico stood frozen in his spot without any customers behind him. "So this is your new bookshop?" His eyes roamed. "Interesting."

She scoffed. "You're very observant, but yes. Some of us can achieve things in spite of our past. If you'll excuse me." Angie rushed away into the staff room at the back of the shop. Her face sweated and her breathing accelerated, the room stifling her. She couldn't stop shaking. Why did he have to come in here and ruin her day?

Chapter 2

THE DILEMMA

E nrico rested on the sofa, his mind on Angie. He couldn't believe she was a businesswoman, and how much she had changed since high school. He remembered her back in school when she was overweight, wore shabby clothing, had a bad haircut with split ends, and wore braces. She had come a long way with her sense of confidence and achievement.

The television screen showed a morbid love scene causing him to shut his eyes. Love stories were not his thing. Not a moment too soon, he heard a loud, familiar voice and opened his eyes.

His mother, Valentina, shouted from the kitchen. "Stella, I want you down here. I need help with the lasagne. Zia Anna and Zio Pietro are coming for dinner."

A few seconds later, his sister replied. "But I'm busy, Mum. I have to study."

Enrico watched his mother, who stood with her hands on her hips, waiting, as if Stella would magically appear. She always took her time whenever they called her from downstairs.

His mother's dark brown eyes under her wrinkled brow could terrorise anyone into bowing to her wishes. She was short with a chubby build and attractive at fifty-two years of age. He loved his mother, but she could challenge anyone at the best of times.

"You come down here now. My back's playing up so I need you to help."

About ten seconds later, Stella called out. "Okay, Mum. I'm coming. Just give me a second." Her second would most likely turn into thirty minutes.

His mother headed towards her son. "Why do you look so worried, Enrico?" She touched her son's arm. "Is it work?"

He pressed his lips together, fighting the images of Angie's glare when she spotted him. He wasn't welcome in her store and he didn't blame her. "No work's fine. I...I saw someone from the past."

She clasped her hands together. "And who would that be?"

He puffed. "Do you remember Angie from school?"

His mother nodded. "The girl whose mother was an alcoholic, picking her up half-drunk a few times?"

"Yes, that's her. Well, she owns a bookshop, and I went in there today and bought a couple of books." He had discovered her bookshop two weeks earlier, but had only found the courage to go in there today.

"Right. So did you two get along in high school?"

"Not exactly, but I don't plan on seeing her again. It's probably for the best." Looking back now, he wasn't proud of how he had treated her, but he couldn't change the past.

His mother looked at him questioningly. "Speaking of schools, have you decided to be a part of your school reunion?"

More recently, his friend, Lorenzo, asked him to join a school reunion committee. Lorenzo was friends with Jenna, who was the organiser.

"I might, but work's been a bit busy, so I'll see if I can make the time. Lorenzo mentioned they haven't sorted out where to have the meetings yet. It's still in the planning stages."

Stella came down the stairs. She was tall, slim, and toned, and believed that a single cracker contained too many calories. She thrived on diets and read loads of health articles and magazines, which pepped her up. Her towering height accentuated her trim and taut body, and her long brown-black hair waved about as she came down the stairs. "Sounds cool, bro. What's the schedule?"

Enrico lifted his body off the couch, rubbing his thigh. "The first meeting is in a couple of weeks, then they're every fortnight for the next seven months. But I don't know if I have the time for a committee for all those months."

Stella peered at Enrico, her bright blue eyes becoming a shade darker. "Mum, I need to talk to Enrico. Why don't you start on the dough, and I will be right there?"

His mother waved her away in exasperation. "Fine, but hurry up."

She turned back to her brother. "Enrico, I overheard you talking to Mum about Angie. Isn't that the girl you bullied back in high school?" Stella's eyes lingered in the distance.

His cheeks burned. "It was a long time ago, Stella, and something I would rather forget? Why are you bringing it up?"

"I don't know. I am curious about her bookshop. I might just go visit. What do you think? I could use a book or two."

Enrico sighed. "Why? You don't need to go in there. Besides, I won't see her again. I got the books I wanted, and next time I'll buy my books online."

"That's a cop-out, bro. It is her business, and we should be supporting it."

Enrico drew back. He made a mistake going into the bookshop. The way Angie looked at him with daggers in her eyes made him want to leave as soon as he got in there. He shouldn't have gone into her bookshop, knowing she would hate him with a passion. But he was curious about Angie.

His father, Giovanni, would have advised him to take a stand and face his fears. If only his father, a senior detective, was still around. He died several years ago, and Enrico had been watching over his family ever since. He hadn't made the right choices back when he was in Year 12, and he wanted to make up for the way he treated Angie.

A shout from the kitchen reverberated in his ears. "Stella, in here. Now."

Stella got up from the stool. "You should see Angie again and apologise for the way you treated her. You were a jackass, but I still love your sorry arse."

"I love you, too." His sister walked towards the kitchen with a slouch. He didn't need to visit Angie again. She hated him and he had satisfied his curiosity.

Chapter 3

CHANGE OF HEART

Angie breezed through her Carlton townhouse and took off her jacket. She placed it on the clothes hook and walked the narrow walkway to her bedroom. Piles of clothing lay on the floor and a hairbrush rested on the corner of her bed. Closing the beige curtain, Angie put on a crop top underneath her tracksuit. She wanted to head to the local gym for a quick workout after eating a light meal.

She wandered over to the kitchen and swung open the freezer to get a frozen meal when her brother, Jimmy, strolled inside.

"Hey, Angie."

She turned towards him, his dark eyes growing dimmer. His large hands threaded through his dark brown crop-style haircut.

"Hi, Jimmy. Are you okay?"

He hesitated. "Sure." Angie heated her frozen meal, waiting for the ping of the microwave oven then slamming the door. Jimmy sighed. "Oh, come on. Not frozen food again. I bought us tender T-bone steak."

She chewed her food then looked up at him. "I'm going to the gym while I'm still motivated to go. Tomorrow night we can have the steak. Would you like a fish cake?"

He sat on the table with his arms crossed, his eyes focusing away from her as if he was in his own little world. "No, and I've heard that same old story many times." He swallowed. "So how's the bookshop going?"

Her body energised as she dug into the food then took a sip of water. "Not great. I have to find other ways of increasing sales, but I don't know what to do. I started to sell loads of books in the beginning, but these last couple of months have been dead quiet." She had a thought. "Has Jack mentioned anything about expanding his woodwork business?" He looked pensive. "Do you know whether he plans to use the building next door to the bookshop?"

Jimmy shook his head. "Didn't he tell you that you could use the space for more books or a cafe? It was meant for you."

"I don't know, Jimmy. I can't afford to buy more stock so it's pointless to have that space."

"If Jack doesn't decide to use it in the future, you'll come up with something. You always do, Angie."

Angie frowned, not wanting to ruminate about her failing business. Packing up her food scraps, she took another sip of water and fetched her gym bag from the grey two-seater sofa. Throw pillows fell on the floor, but she left them there. Jimmy put the pillows back in their rightful place and tidied up the beige curtains, which had been messed up by Angie's gym bag. Cleaning was the last thing on her priority list. "And everything's okay with your course?"

He nodded. "I'm loving the course. I'm starting my placement at a youth drop-in centre in the next couple of months. I can't wait."

Angie smiled at Jimmy's choice of career in youth work. He thrived on helping people with his empathetic and understanding nature.

"Sounds interesting." She smiled and wrapped him in a big bear hug. "I'll catch you soon, Jimmy. I need to burn off those calories."

"Wait." She changed her stance and put down her gym bag.

Jimmy inched his way towards her. "Do you remember Jenna Dangles from high school?" Her mind flashed back to the shameful memories back then. She nodded. She'd been kind to Angie, one of the few former schoolmates who had. "Well, Jenna's sister, Dina, and I have recently become friends, and she mentioned how Jenna's started organising a school reunion. She's struggling to find more people to join the planning committee for the reunion. Apparently, someone pulled out at the last minute, and no-one wants to commit. Why don't you join?"

Angie winced. She didn't want to dredge up the horrid memories of high school. Why should she be a part of it? "I don't think so, Jimmy. I am pretty busy with the bookshop six days a week, so I don't think I'd have the time to commit."

Jimmy approached and touched her shoulder. "I understand how bad it was at school, but aren't you the one who always told me to help others in need? Contribute to the community? I think if you can confront the past, you'll be able to move forward. Take on the challenge. Isn't it what you drum into my head?"

Angie's breathing turned erratic. "I have moved forward, Jimmy."

"No, you haven't. I think, if you can get to the source of the problem, namely your school life, you won't have that over your head and you'll stop underestimating the kind of person you are. I know the bullying still bothers you. It needs to be faced, Angie."

She knew he was right, but she had closed that chapter of her life. Why rehash it? Angie had to admit that, in spite of all she achieved, a part of her body housed a deep sense of emptiness.

"And they're wanting to find a venue that is not expensive and has space.I guess the committee has a limited budget. Maybe you could offer the bookstore? It would bring in more income and get people there."

She angled her head, her mind churning at the possibility. Could she offer up her bookshop as a venue and bring in some extra revenue? They had all that space next door. It could be a good idea to bring in more revenue. They could rent out the shop and the space next door for events or meetings. She could focus on the bigger picture and see it as a business transaction. "Fine, Jimmy. I'll offer up the bookstore as a space, but only if I get a say on how the space is used. And a damage deposit."

"It sounds great, Angie. What a great idea. I'll tell Dina to get Jenna to ring you."

As Angie was leaving the gym, her phone buzzed in her bag. She dug into the gym bag and glimpsed the caller ID—a number she didn't recognise. She answered the call. "Hello."

"Angie...Is that you?"

The voice sounded familiar. "Yes, it's Angie. Who is this?"

"It's Jenna Dangles from high school. Do you remember me?"

She slouched as she made her way back to her car and entered. "Hi, Jenna. I do remember you. My brother, Jimmy mentioned being friends with your sister."

"Yes, Dina did tell me that. Anyway, I'm the main organiser of the reunion committee, and Jimmy mentioned you wanted to offer up your bookshop as a venue for the reunion celebration?"

Her hands shook slightly. "That's right." She could use the extra money and possibly have a side business to help pay for the bank loan. She didn't want to default on the loan, and if things didn't improve, she would.

"We do have funding to pay you for the venue, but I'll check it out and let you know. Now someone on the committee decided to pull out at the last minute. I haven't had much luck finding another committee member, and we do need one more. I would really appreciate one more person helping out. Would you be interested, Angie?"

Focus on the big picture, she thought. She'd always been the type to help out, and if she was offering the bookshop for a venue, Angie needed to be on the committee to make sure they choose it, and that decorations and activities didn't risk the store. "If I'm possibly having the venue at my bookstore, I really should help out."

"Great." She paused. "Do you have a space we could use for our meetings? Our home is getting renovated at the moment and I haven't asked anyone else yet. It'll give me a chance to check out the space. But I will understand if you say no, Angie. I can ask someone else."

She did have the space. Clenching her fists, she pushed down her nerves. "Sure."

"You're amazing, Angie. Thank you." She coughed. "I feel really bad I wasn't friends with you back in high school. I know you had your own friends, but I wanted to do more for you, and I think I should've stood up for you against those bullies. I was too gutless."

"That's ridiculous, Jenna. I remember you did give them a piece of your mind on a couple of occasions. Besides, you had no control over the pranks they pulled on me or the words they used. You had your own life and there is no need to make it up to me."

"Thanks for saying that, but I should've done more. Anyway, would next Wednesday night at seven be okay with you?"

"Sure. Not a problem. I can text you my address."

"I will let the others know. Thanks again, Angie. You're a life-saver."

She ended the call with a heavy heart, wondering if she made the right decision.

Chapter 4

A SOUR PAST

E nrico ended the call on his phone after talking to his friend, Lorenzo, who was also a policeman. He decided to join the reunion committee, and Jenna mentioned that the meetings were now going to be held at Angie's bookstore. He assumed she'd be on the committee if she was offering up her store as a meeting place. So much for staying out of her way.Enrico decided to join the committee as a way of helping out a few caterer friends of his to establish their business, and what better way than to give one of them the reunion to cater for? Although he would have to make a choice between them, so a couple of them would miss out. He was also well-known within his local community of Brunswick and thrived on getting involved in any kind of event. Working on the reunion committee was also a way to give back to his local area after the way he behaved in high school.

Enrico enjoyed being a policeman to instil justice, but the flashes of his past still lingered in his mind. The reunion committee could be the event that would give him some closure over the past, and he was looking forward to the experience. He wasn't sure how he'd be interacting with Angie, but he was a changed man and he had to push through his guilt.As his mind turned back to Angie, he realised one thing. As bad as he had been back in high school, she hadn't been easy to like back then either. She had been opinionated and distant, as if she didn't care about anything. He focused back on the present and got ready for the first reunion meeting at Angie's bookstore in Fitzroy.

Walking out of the house, he entered his car, drove to Fitzroy, and parked by the kerb. He dreaded seeing Angie again.

Heading to the back of the bookshop, he dodged a few people on the street and made his way to the door. He rang the doorbell and waited for a few minutes, wondering if anyone heard it. He shuffled his feet along the ground and took a deep breath. When the door opened wide, their eyes locked and Angie glared at him. Obviously, it wasn't such a great idea that he'd decided to join the committee.

Oh, Christ! Enrico! You have got to be kidding me. This arrogant jerk was on the committee. Why didn't Jenna mention anything?

"What are you doing here?" Angie asked.

His face warmed. "I'm on the reunion committee. It was a last-minute change, but I told my friend, Lorenzo, to let Jenna know."

She crossed her arms and left the door partially ajar, spotting Jenna behind him. She was a short woman with friendly blue eyes and black, bob style hair. "Hi Jenna."

Jenna looked at Enrico then Angie. "Hi guys." She whispered in her ear. "I am so sorry. I didn't know he was coming. But maybe it's time you sorted things out? He is a changed man, and I should know, his friend, Lorenzo, is also a close friend of my husband."

Enrico must've heard the comment. "Didn't Lorenzo mention I decided to join?"

Jenna shook her head. "No, he must've forgotten." She frowned. "Let's get started."

Angie opened the door wider and let them inside the staff room which had two red leather couches, a kitchenette, a table with four timber chairs, and a computer with desk space.

As Enrico sat awkwardly on the couch, Angie took out jugs of water with glasses and set them on the table. Then she brought out a tray of cheese, dips, and crackers. Her hands were shaking as she ignored the man she loathed and focused on ushering the last of the committee into the back. One by one, the rest of the group entered the back of the shop. When everyone had gathered, Jenna introduced Angie to the six people in the room, some smiling and two others with blank expressions. "You remember Gina, Ray, Tim, and Susie."

"Good to see you all again." Angie nodded. A deep old wound ignited fury at the way Gina ignored her, and how Ray pretended he hadn't been equally as vicious as the other bullies. Gina obviously hadn't changed.

As the remainder of the group took their seats, the only empty seat was beside Enrico.

She took the seat but sat motionlessly. In the corner of her eye, she could see Enrico's gaze fixed on her. If she'd known the bullying group would be part of the committee, she wouldn't have agreed to this. Perhaps Jenna wasn't as kind as Angie thought.

With clenched teeth, Angie directed her gaze to Jenna sorting out documents. Bile rose in her throat at the way Gina gawked with her dark-brown eyes, threading her fingers through her red hair. The black tight-fitted t-shirt displayed her cleavage and tight jeans showed her buxom curves. What she possessed in beauty, she lacked in warmth and personality. She'd been Enrico's girlfriend back in Year 12, and Angie wondered if they were still a couple. Not that she cared. They were welcome to each other.

"Let's get started." Jenna straightened in her seat. "First of all, let's discuss housekeeping rules. We'll meet here fortnightly or every three weeks, but the days might change. Depending on progress, we might be able to catch up virtually as it gets closer to the seven months. We will endeavour to have the reunion by early December. Later than that, and people might be away on holidays." She looked at Angie. "Angie's been kind enough to organise snacks and to offer us this space. Thanks, Angie." Angie smiled, then Jenna turned over a page. "I've spoken to the school alumni and funding should be arranged. I have a handout with all the tasks." She distributed a document, and each member passed the paper over to the next person.

"You have a cosy place here, Angie," said Susie, who was petite with black, curly hair.

"Thanks, Susie," said Angie. She remembered that Susie had been pleasant enough but had had her own personal issues in school.

"It must be exciting to own a bookshop," said Tim who was tall with dark eyes and red-brown hair. She smiled in his direction. He had been a great support for Susie when her parents divorced and hadn't much noticed Angie was being bullied. But he had been friendly towards Angie.

Enrico faced her with a cool stare and placed the document into her hand.

Grudgingly, Angie took the paper from Enrico. She must've left the heat on. Angie felt uncomfortably warm and shifted in her seat.

"I'd like nominations for the following tasks: we need a communication team to set up a reunion website or private page and an email list to notify classmates. We need an events team to enquire about possible venues and catering. Oh, and before I forget, Angie did suggest we could possibly use her empty building space next door and the back of this shop as a possible reunion venue. We can check it out another time. We also need an activities team to plan the music and entertainment. I'll manage the finances, ticket sales, and budget. Okay, let's have show of hands for what you'd like to organise."

"Okay, so Gina, you're wanting to pair with Ray for the emails, website, marketing kind of stuff. And Susie, you're happy to work with Tim to arrange the music, entertainment and decorating, and finally..." Jenna mouthed a silent sorry to Angie. "And as Enrico knows his community with contacts in the restaurant industry, I guess the last pair will need to focus on venues or planning out Angie's space next door and catering. That's Angie and Enrico. Any questions?"

Angie stilled, stared into her lap, briefly closing her eyes, sensing Enrico's eyes boring into her.

"Okay, talk strategy with your partner and help yourself to Angie's amazing snack trays." Jenna poured herself a glass of water.

Angie ignored the strong cologne—he must have bathed in. The awkward silence caused her to watch others bow down in discussions while Enrico sat like a pompous creep. He sat cross-armed and stiff, his eyes directed towards Gina and Ray.

He avoided her eyes with his posture straight, but at least he broke the silence. "I am checking out my contacts for places we can visit for catering. We can discuss a menu and plan out how you want to arrange your venue next door, if we decide to use the space."

She pursed her lips and held her elbows away from her body. "Whatever, but I'm happy working on my own."

He frowned. "We need to be working in pairs, Angie."

She sighed "Why? When we'd most likely work better on our own. I didn't even know you'd be on the committee."

He clenched his hands. "We'll have to visit the venues together, and as I said, work as a team."

Angie scoffed. "Well, that is unfortunate." She gave him a mocking smile.

His body stiffened, his expression cold and hard. "Why are you being difficult?"

Her face infused with heat and her pulse sped up. How dare he say that when he was the one who had bullied her? But she recovered from it in a way with the help of her mother, Charlotte and stepfather, Jack. Enrico had no right to be rude. "You know what? We do not need to work together. I will do my work and you do yours. Suits me fine."

"If that's what you want."

She wanted to slap the jerk and ignored the others watching their exchange. "Hmm. It is, so don't make a big deal of it."

Gina intervened by touching Enrico seductively on his thigh. She looked daggers at her. "Angie, dear. Would you mind keeping your ice queen comments to yourself? Some of us are trying to work."

Angie ignored her, but rather focused on Jenna who wandered around, offering the cheese, dip, and crackers.

Jenna faced the group. "How is everyone doing? Making progress?"

Susie replied. "I have a few friends in mind who might do the DJ work. I'll speak to them."

"Great. Anyone else?"

Gina and Ray began to hash out their plan with Jenna.

Angie's mind flashed back to Gina bullying her the most, at least at a verbal level, while Enrico, Ray, and their other friends taunted her less often but were still damaging, given their group pranks. She did not need to put up with any of them.

This was her bookstore after all. Angie moved her chair and sat near Susie and Tim. She would handle the venue. Enrico could handle catering. They didn't need to work together on that. He could stay on his side with Gina and Ray, and she could ignore him and save her business.

Chapter 5

A FAMILY AFFAIR

A few days later, Angie sat in her car with Jimmy in the passenger seat as they drove the busy streets to visit their mother and stepfather. She turned off the motor in the driveway, but her body wouldn't budge. The events from Wednesday night dominated her mind, and she had a deep-seated need to hit a punching bag at the gym to release her rage. Preferably, she would've liked to punch Enrico.

Jimmy pursed his lips, his eyes squinting at her lack of motion. "What's with you, sis? Are we going in or not?"

Angie took a deep breath and fought off the images of her past which still troubled her. Not only in school, but at home too. Her father abandoned them when she was only twelve and Jimmy was six. He was never around anyway before then—gambling away what little money they had. She focused back on the present and nodded. "Let's go, Jimmy. I'm fine."

She exited the car and made her way towards an average-sized brick veneer home with a landscaped garden, displaying low scrub, fernery, and various-sized conifers. Hanging plants grew beside a double-frosted front door behind a security gate. The worn concrete path was slightly cracked and uneven. She turned to Jimmy and smiled, a warmth as always settling in her heart for the brother she loved dearly. He was her rock, had kept her sane over the years, and she didn't know what she would've done without him. He rang the doorbell then put his hand over his mouth. "Oh, Christ! Your meeting a few days ago. I forgot all about it. Was it upsetting for you?"

She remained tight-lipped. "We'll talk about it later. Like I said, I'm fine." She put on a forced grin as the front door opened.

Her mother smiled from ear to ear. "Angie, Jimmy, I'm so glad you both made it. It has been a while. Come in." She hugged them both.

The last two years had been kind to her mother since ceasing alcohol. She had smooth skin and a slim build with glossy, strawberry-blonde hair. She wore a loose cotton t-shirt and black jeans which were slightly ripped at the seams. She appeared younger than her forty-four years.

The house had high ceilings, a narrow walkway with a full-length mirror, and a clothes hook near a large bookcase. Her mother led her to the living room with black plush carpeting underneath a brown leather sofa, a huge SMART TV surrounded by another bookshelf, a timber coffee table, and several foot stools opposite the TV.

"Have a seat," said her mother. "Would you like a drink before dinner?"

Angie's body relaxed as she focused on the moment. "No, I'm fine, Mum." Jimmy shook his head. "Later for me, Mum." He searched the room. "Where's Jack?"

Her mother rubbed one thumb over another. She picked up a glass of juice resting on the coffee table and took a sip. "He was finishing up something, but he's coming."

Moments later, Jack wandered into the living room. "Hello, guys. Great to see you. It's been far too long since we've had dinner together." He shook Jimmy's hand and wrapped his arms around Angie. He was average height with a solid but slim build. His hair was grey on the sides and dark on top. His blue eyes exuded warmth.

Her mother and Jack got both children talking about their lives, and Angie always had an amazing time with her parents. She had grown close with her mother since she stopped drinking and worked hard to remain sober.

"Okay, let's go and eat. I've made your favourite. Lasagne."

Jimmy nodded. "Love it, Mum. Thanks."

She prodded him into the kitchen with the others behind. "I know, Jimmy. I know. It gives me comfort to know you enjoy my cooking."

Angie and Jimmy sat side by side at the kitchen table while her mother took the lasagne from the oven, the delicious meaty and spicy aroma filling the room. She always liked her mother's cooking.

Setting down the plate of lasagne, her mother set down a salad and a tray of vegetables while Jack took out a bottle of orange juice.

Jack put the bottle on the table. "I have orange juice but, if you'd like something else, we have soft drink or pineapple juice." Both in agreement, Jack poured them each a glass. He refilled his own and poured pineapple juice into her mother's glass.

They devoured their lasagne in silence until Angie broke the quiet. "So how's the custom carpentry business doing?"

Her mother put down her fork. "It's doing well. The accounts for the business show it's profitable."

Jack stroked her mother's cheek. "Charlotte's amazing with the accounts. If it wasn't for her numbers acumen, I wouldn't be able to manage those profit and loss sheets—which is why we make a great team. I'm the hands-on person and your mum's the numbers woman." He winked at her and her mother blushed.

She shoved him lovingly on the shoulder. "Oh, stop it, Jack. Flattery will get you everywhere, though."

Angie gripped her fork, a sense of envy permeating her stomach. She wished for that kind of love. Would she ever be loved the way her parents loved each other? Her mother worked hard to build a good life, fighting her alcoholism and overcoming Angie and Jimmy's dad leaving them.

Jack put down his glass, facing Angie and Jimmy. "So what's new with both of you? It has been at least a week since we last spoke."

Jimmy spoke up first. "Angie's part of her high school reunion committee."

Her mother's face paled. "Oh!"

Jack's eyes widened. "Tell us more about that, Angie. It sounds intriguing."

If only Jimmy kept his mouth shut. Now she would have to open up about that arrogant man, Enrico. She wanted to throttle the guy.

Chapter 6

WOUNDS

Angie fought the urge to rush out of there. The reunion committee brought up the past. She gripped her glass as images flashed in her mind. She remembered her mother stumbling a few times when picking her up from school. Another time, she slurred inappropriate words to a teacher during a parent-teacher interview. Students teased her about the countless times her mother showed up drunk at school events. Angie opted to catch the bus home in the end, minimizing the embarrassment. Her mother managed to sweet-talk her way out of the school calling child protection. If her mother hadn't recovered, Angie wouldn't have had a relationship with her.

Over the years, Angie compensated for her mother's disease by focusing on her studies to ensure she achieved her goals. She adapted to looking after herself and Jimmy when her mother was too drunk to cook meals or do the shopping. Her father would work from one job to the next and gamble his money away. He had anger issues too, but mainly directed it at her mother. Her mother's drinking became worse after Angie's father left. Her father passed away a few years ago. Her mother and Jack had been married for the past three years. It was the love of a good man in Jack who helped her fight the disease, and she hoped her mother stayed the course of her journey, in spite of a couple of relapses. These were due to coping as a single mother with their limited finances, and her biological father's death. In spite of their issues, her mother had still grieved the loss.

"Angie? Tell us about this committee," her mother said.

"Nothing much to say, really." She recounted the course of events, noticing her mother's hands begin to tremble. Her mother understood too well what it had been like for her children.

"I know I've said it before, Angie, but I am sorry for what I put you through. That clique in school always gave you a hard time because of me." Her mother rested her hand against her chest, fixing her gaze on Angie.

Jack gave her mother a tender caress. "It was the group responsible for their actions and words, not you. I'm sure Angie doesn't blame you, Charlotte."

Angie fought back a wave of heaviness in her chest. She had blamed her mother at the time. She wanted her mother never to relapse again, but it was a risk she needed to prepare for. "Oh, Mum. You weren't responsible for the bullying. It is Enrico who angers me. He is so arrogant, and now he's on this reunion committee to rub salt in my wounds. Even a couple of others from that group are on the committee: Gina and Ray. They did unforgivable things. It wasn't really about you, Mum. It was me they hated."

Jimmy intervened. "Enrico might be different now."

Angie shook her head. "But that's the thing, Jimmy. He is still superficial, I'm sure. As far as I'm concerned, I have to think of my business and work with him." She explained her business idea and how she wanted to use her building and bookstore for the venue. "I doubt he's changed, but I'm not going to be a baby about it."

Her mother gave her a reassuring smile. "Oh, honey. If only you had known Enrico would be on this committee before you signed on, then you wouldn't have to go through this again. But I'm sure you can make this work. You have achieved so much with your business and your new home. Do not sell yourself short, Angie."

Jack gave her a thumbs up. "You've got this, girl. Don't let those guys put you back there in school. You can get through it. If you under-estimate yourself, they get the upper hand." He beamed. "And I am so happy you're using the building we bought for you. At least, this way, you're expanding it in your own way. It's a great idea, Angie."

"Thanks, Jack." Angie wanted to believe that she had achieved a lot in her twenty-seven years, but the darkness of her school life filled her core. It still clouded her mother, too. "I'll be fine. I can get through it for the next seven months. We can work virtually together later, I'm sure." She had to get through it for the sake of her business.

After finishing their meal and washing up, Jimmy's voice jolted her from a distance as she turned around. "Hurry up, Angie. I want to watch the last bit of a sports program."

She dashed to the front door after kissing her parents and waving goodbye.

Chapter 7

CAFE MOMENT

E nrico sat in his garage and banged a nail from one plank of wood into another. He was attempting to make a bookshelf for the study area and almost nailed his thumb. He was distracted, his mind flicking back to Angie. He still couldn't believe he had to work with her when she had so much attitude towards him. Not that he blamed her, but hadn't she realised he was not the same person anymore? Why couldn't she live in the moment?

She would be attractive if it wasn't for her self-entitled attitude. She acted like an ice-queen who had little to no emotions, and it drove him to frustration.

Enrico opened a tin of varnish and picked up a brush. He dipped it into the tin and painted it over the planks of wood. His arms ached, but he kept spreading the varnish over the bookshelf. Once he finished, he packed up and washed his hands.

He walked into his bedroom and debated whether to ring Angie about a list of catering venues they could visit. He doubted she would accept anything constructive after the meeting, given her anger towards him. It was a Sunday so she had to be home. He didn't want to see her again, but Jenna insisted that seven months was cutting it fine to plan the school reunion.

Oh, let me get this over with. He retrieved his mobile phone, placed the call, and waited. His hands got clammy, likely from the physical work he'd been doing. Why was she taking so long to answer the phone? He shifted his feet on the carpet and gasped when he heard her voice. "Angie. It's Enrico." Silence. "Hello. Are you there?"

"I'm here."

"I don't know if Jenna mentioned that she tentatively approved of your bookshop and building next door as the reunion venue, but she still needs to run it by the group."

"I got the message."

He ignored the ice in her voice. "I have a list of caterers we can visit for the reunion so we can sample the food. I have a few friends with catering businesses, and we can choose the best samples of food later. Are you free this afternoon?" He waited at least six seconds before she replied. He didn't have all day.

"It is last minute but I should be. Where do you want to meet?"

"How about in the city? In front of Flinders Street Station, close to the corner of Elizabeth and Swanston Streets. The catering venues are within walking distance."

She sighed. "Fine. What time?"

"Make it two o'clock." She ended the call before he had a chance to say goodbye. With a shake of his head, he put his phone away, dreading this meeting.

Enrico stood in front of the station, his eyes wandering around the clusters of people walking in and out of the station and the surrounding stores. The autumn sunshine warmed the back of his neck as he kept thinking he'd seen Angie when it was only someone who resembled her. He pushed down his fury and checked his phone. She was ten minutes late and he wondered if he'd been stood up. He watched couples holding hands and groups of friends laughing amongst themselves, while young families ran after toddlers heading for the steps.

He rubbed at the middle of his forehead. He forgot to breathe for a second when Angie finally appeared wearing a tight denim skirt and a fitted white blouse which displayed a long neck and tanned upper chest. Her long, brown hair with burgundy highlights flowed around her flawless skin. What was wrong with him? She might've been attractive, but she wasn't his friend.

Up close, her green eyes squinted, and he focused on her full rosy lips. He hadn't noticed her features much the other night at the reunion meeting, but even so, he was damned if he'd give her the upper hand in this working relationship.

"Enrico." She held her head high, barely fixing her eyes on him.

"Angie. Let's go. The venue's a five-minute walk." He was suddenly parched but pushed the feeling down. He had a mission, and the sooner he was done with this partnership the better. "It's at a cafe downstairs that has an exclusive bar in the back."

Her fingers grazed his hand as they crossed the road towards the exclusive bar and he wished she'd say something. She'd been cold and aloof in high school, but that didn't mean she couldn't say two words to him. He pushed on ahead until they reached the bar and swung open the door to be greeted by a tall waiter sporting a moustache.

"Table for two?"

He shook his head firmly. "No. I have an appointment to speak with the owner, Jonathan. We're a few minutes late. The name's Enrico."

He knit his brows. "Right. He had to step out for a half-hour, but you're welcome to wait and have a coffee here. We have a table free in the back."

Enrico slouched, facing Angie. "Do you want coffee? The next appointment is in an hour so we have time."

Angie nodded. "Fine."

The waiter showed them to their table and they sat opposite one another. He took their orders of a cafe latte for Angie and espresso for Enrico.

The silence was unnerving as Angie crossed her arms stiffly. "So what do you know about this caterer?"

He shrugged. "I know the owner. I helped him out with a disgruntled customer." Angie stared into her lap, looking bored. "They have a courtyard, a bar, and a full kitchen that serves tapas and finger foods. Jonathan's planning a menu for us out back we can try."

"We're here for the food, so I don't need you to describe the venue when I've offered up my place. Or did you forget that?" Her eyes wandered to patrons coming inside.

"I am just trying to make conversation." Enrico fidgeted, his chest tightening. Damn, he was at a loss for words. The energy between them was dense. *Say something, you idiot!* "What have you been doing since school?"

Angie shifted. "Listen, Enrico. You don't have to be nice. We both know that you and I don't really want to be here."

Before he had a chance to respond, the waiter brought their coffees and left. It was going to be a long afternoon.

Chapter 8

MISTRUST

Angie's back ached as she sat on the hard-backed chair. Enrico's eyes lingered on her as if he didn't know what to say. She ignored the flutter in her stomach at his presence and the gaze from those clear blue eyes. His lips pressed hard together and he fiddled with his collar. His shirt stretched across a taut chest, and several strands of hair escaped the V at his neck. The tight jeans he wore showed his toned legs. What was she doing?

"Why don't we address the elephant in the room? We both didn't want to be working together, but I have the contacts and you have to love food, right? We can try to make the best out of a crappy situation. If you give me a chance, you'll see I have grown up since high school. You want this reunion to do well. After all, we are using your store as the venue. Your business reputation is on the line."

She jutted her chin. "Whatever you say."

He scoffed. "Charming."

Angie sighed. "You're right. That's why I am here. My business reputation is on the line, and I won't have a bully like you ruin one of the few good things in my life. Let's just choose a caterer, get through this reunion, and go our separate ways."

They both drank their coffees in silence until Jonathan arrived, approached them, and greeted them both with a handshake.

"Hi Enrico. Good to see you again, man." He towered over them and had a crew cut. Enrico introduced Angie. "Nice to meet you, Angie. Come on through. Now I know Enrico mentioned you wanted to try out the food, but in case things go pear-shaped and you decide on us for the venue too, I can show you around. See it for future reference." He led them to the bar out back and gave them the grand tour. The room had high beamed walls, windows that overlooked a courtyard filled with assorted greenery, stone walls, a range of tables and stools lined across the bar, and a spacious, tiled floor for dancing or talking.

Angie listened to his spiel about the full range of kitchen facilities, pricing, brand of cuisine, drink options, their decorations policy, and musical equipment. She wanted to use her own space and didn't want to be cajoled into using a different venue. Had Enrico brought her here with the intention of changing the reunion venue?

Jonathan ushered them towards a table. "I'll get you the first course." He walked away with a curt nod."

Angie sat with her hands clasped in front of her, avoiding his eyes as she waited. She steeled herself to confront him. "Are you looking at alternative venues?"

Enrico drew back as if not expecting the question. "There's no harm in looking at other possibilities. Just in case."

Angie swallowed hard. "In case of what?"

He took a deep breath and brushed a strand away from his eyes. "Listen. I know Jenna tentatively approved your bookshop, but your space needs a bit of work to get it prepped. I thought we could look at venues that also do catering. No harm in that."

Angie scoffed. "Are you serious right now? You haven't changed one bit. You're still trying to control me and have the upper hand."

Jonathan brought a large tray of appetisers and set them in the middle of the table with two small plates for Enrico and Angie. "We have here the pre-dinner food, comprising asparagus and crème fraiche, vol-au-vents, spinach and bacon pin-wheels, assorted dips and home-made crackers, and Oyster Kilpatrick."

"Thank you. It smells good." Angie wasn't in the mood to eat, but she made the effort. There was too much at stake. She picked up a vol-au-vent and bit into the cheesy, crunchy texture which was full of flavour. Enrico scooped up an oyster and used a small fork to devour it.

Enrico smiled at his friend. "You've excelled again, Jonathan. Thanks, mate."

"Only the best for my good friend. Enjoy."

After eating samples of the pre-dinner snacks in awkward silence, Enrico broke the ice. "We've got two more catering venues around the corner, and then we're done for today. If we like any one of these caterers, we can make a shortlist. But I have a few more on my list, so we should keep looking. We still have time to choose one."

She didn't bother telling him how much she hated his need for control. He was trying to take over with the venue when he had no idea how much her business idea needed to work. "Fine."

After finishing off a couple more courses, Angie stood up when Jonathon returned. "That was amazing food, Jonathan. I appreciate your time."

His eyes lit up. "The pleasure was all mine, Angie." He turned to Enrico. "Check out the other venues and let me know what you decide."

He shook hands with Jonathon. "We'll get together soon, man. I'll be in touch, and thanks again. But please don't hold it against me if we decide on someone else as it's a team decision."

Jonathan nodded. "I understand, man. See you soon."

Enrico stepped outside. "What did you really think of the food?"

Angie walked ahead of him. "Great.""

On their way to the next building, a man selling flowers in a basket approached Enrico. "How about a lovely rose for your girlfriend over here."

Enrico flinched. "No, thank you." He kept walking but the man followed them.

"But she is beautiful and has dark, troubled eyes. I can see she needs cheering up. Why not give her a rose?"

Enrico glared. "She is not my girlfriend, okay. And she's fine. Thank you." Enrico glanced in her direction.

The man got the message and winked at Angie who grinned back at the man. She bought a rose from the man and thanked him kindly. She caught up with Enrico, her steps dreamy and slow as she savoured the moment with her nose stuffed in the flower, inhaling with a soft smile on her lips. The flower and kind man were the only blessings in this entire trip. Though, she had to admit, the food they had tried so far was impressive. She expected sports bars and fast food from Enrico. When her eyes lifted to his, he was staring at her with an expression of shock. She lowered the pink flower to her side.

"What?"

"Nothing." Enrico frowned. "This way." He turned and walked to the next restaurant without looking back.

After trying out more food, they walked towards the final destination for the day which was closer to Melbourne Central.

Angie's phone rang in her bag. "I have to take this. It might be important."

He hid his disappointment. "Fine. Go ahead."

She answered the phone. "Hmm. Sure. I'll be there in about half an hour. No worries. Bye." Angie avoided his eyes. "I have to go. My neighbour and friend sometimes asks me to babysit his daughter when he works on the occasional Sunday. He is a single father and can't get anyone else today." She put her phone back in her bag.

He sighed. "What about the food? You can't expect me to make the decision on my own."

Angie dug her nails into her bag. "I am sure your little brain can work it out. I'll see you around. Let me know about next time." She rushed ahead to the train station and didn't turn back, but she sensed his eyes boring into her back.

She pondered their exchange, still viewing him as an arrogant jerk who wanted to control her. As if he couldn't make a decision about catering. Didn't he have taste? Why did he believe they could work together when she hated every ounce of his being? But Angie was always up for the challenge, and she wouldn't let him hurt her as he had in the past. She was no longer that shy, unconfident teenager who masked her pain just to cope.

Chapter 9

APOLOGY

Angie smiled at Gerard. His wife died a year ago, and she'd been babysitting his ten-year-old daughter, Lucinda, since then. In the last year, they'd become fast friends. He had bright green eyes and a solid build, with wavy, brown hair and a burn scar on the right side of his face. He was a handsome man, and as close friends, they often socialised or shared a coffee together.

"I'm sorry for the late notice, but work called and I was their back-up for today. They're understaffed with chefs. I hope you weren't busy."

She shook her head. "No, it was fine. Nothing important." A waste of time, more like it, she thought.

Lucinda's eyes widened as she scurried up to her for a huge hug. "Angie, I missed you." She was a gorgeous little girl with green eyes, shoulder-length blonde hair, and the cutest, chubbiest cheeks.

They pulled apart. "I missed you too, sweetie. So what do you want to do today?"

Lucinda had a fire in her eyes. "We can play Scrabble."

Gerard kissed his daughter. "I have to go now, Luce. You behave for Aunty Angie, okay? I'll be back soon."

He wrapped his arms around her in a friendly hug, then pulled away with a huge smile. "We need to have a meal one night. It's been crazy busy, but I'll make time for you and Maddy. What do you say?"

"Of course. Set the time and date and we'll be there."

He saluted with style and gave her a wink, then blew a kiss to Lucinda who pretended to catch it. "Great. See you later." He headed off and closed the door behind him.

"Okay, girlie. Why don't we go set up the Scrabble set?"

Lucinda clapped. "Yay!"

Later in the night, Angie was in bed looking at something on her phone when her mind turned to Enrico. He had been annoyed with her for skipping out on their meeting. A sense of guilt washed over her, but why should she feel guilty?

She had been helping out a friend in need. She couldn't say no to Gerard because he had suffered, both as a widowed dad and as a child. He had experienced a burn accident as a child only to grow up to have a mother and wife both die from cancer—too many losses in one lifetime to endure.

Angie scrolled through emails, deleting those for the junk folder until her phone vibrated. She answered the call. "Hello." Silence. "Hello?"

"Angie. It's Enrico. Were you sleeping?"

She shifted her body and sat up. "Enrico. No, I wasn't asleep yet. Why are you ringing so late?"

"I wanted to apologise for the way I barked at you when you were trying to help out a friend. I kind of thought about it, and...Well...It was rude."

Her heart skipped a beat from the shock. An apology was the last thing she expected. She didn't need him to apologise. "It's fine. Don't worry about it. I'm a big girl and I can take it."

He sighed. "I wanted to arrange another couple of visits for next Saturday if you're free. Just a thought."

"I can't. I'll be working on Saturday. We could meet Sunday night."

"Okay," said Enrico. He paused. "I'll arrange it for Sunday, and will confirm closer to the date. Goodnight."

"Goodnight." He sounded halfway decent, as if he was human after all, but she was still wary of his motives. As a policeman he had to put on a show and look good in front of his peers and community. Nothing more than that.

Chapter 10

FRIENDLY ADVICE

Angie and Maddy strolled through The Carlton Gardens, which featured the dynamic Royal Exhibition Building, the Melbourne Museum, Imax Cinema, artificial grass tennis courts underneath towering trees, and a children's playground.

Angie and Maddy strolled across sweeping lawns with their range of trees and plants featuring English Oaks, elms, and conifers, alongside flower beds of shrubs and annuals. Lilac and rose fragrances drifted on the lazy breeze. White and purple petals fell to the ground. The occasional petal carried on the breeze flying past the three-tiered water fountain. The gurgle of the water broke the quiet as it cascaded across carved arches and leaves down into the fountain base and back up again. The sunlight washed over her arms and warmed her. Pointed arches of roofs rose above the tops of trees, and delicate wood trim blended with colourful flowers. The clouds in the blue sky were slowly fading, and the sun was smiling down upon them.

Finding a patch of open grass near the fountain, the two women settled down for a short break. Picking at the grass and sipping her bottled water, Angie squinted in the bright sunshine. She fished for the sunglasses in her bag beside her and put them on. Maddy took a sip of her bottled cola then dabbed her mouth with a tissue retrieved from the back pocket of her jeans. It was a Sunday morning and Angie's first day in nature in a while. "So don't you think you should talk to Enrico about the way he treated you?"

"What's the point? It won't change anything. He even suggested we look at other venues when Jenna approved of the bookshop and building next door as a venue. He still wants to control me, Maddy, and it proves he hasn't changed."

"You should talk to him about that. He's probably just looking at other options. I mean, the building next door does need a bit of work, so he might be worried it won't be ready in time." She stared across at passersby.

She shook her head. "No, it's just his need for control. That's all it is, but he won't win this time. He humiliated me at school, Maddy."

"I know he and his friends called you the ice queen and played pranks, but he might be different now."

"He was at least a little civilised last Sunday. He might have a bit of humanity, but he still didn't say anything when Gina called me an ice queen again. It doesn't seem like he has changed much. He was such a jerk in high school." Angie's face reddened.

Maddy edged her way closer to her friend. "I know. He was a jerk in high school, and as much as I tried to fight for you, they went on and on and tormented you. But I wish you had stood up for yourself then, and not pretended it didn't affect you."

Angie swallowed. "You're right. I should have." Her mind drifted. "I remember the times he called me a loser and said that I should have my own show called 'Ugly Angie.' It hurt. He even said I wouldn't amount to anything. That I lack a heart."

Maddy stroked her hand. "I know. They were all bullies, but it's time to clear the air with Enrico. Get it all out in the open so he knows exactly how he made you feel then. It's time to sort this out." She frowned. "He did seem a bit different in the bookshop, so give him the benefit of the doubt. You owe it to yourself to get closure on this, Angie."

"Maybe. I was too late in picking my partner at the first reunion meeting, so I have to work with him."

Maddy gave her a reassuring smile. "It makes sense if he knows good places to cater the reunion while you're responsible for the venue, to work together. Besides, it sounds like you get some good food out of the deal. So when are you seeing him again?"

"We're meeting tonight at Brunetti's."

"Why there?" Maddy scrunched up her nose. "Doesn't seem like a place that would suit for catering the reunion."

Angie was dreading the night, not motivated to see him again. "The venues we need to attend are close by, so he thought we'd have a coffee and chat in between the two appointments."

Maddy nodded. "You can clear the air, but as I said before, you need closure. Time to get the past out into the open. Get his perspective on things."

Angie shook her head. "Possibly."

Maddy rubbed her temple, glancing into the distance. "I should come with you and be the mediator. You cannot leave things unsaid. Enrico being at the committee was a sign. A sign that you need to work on things."

Angie nodded. "Thanks, Maddy. You always stood by me, and I wish I had your spirit back in high school. If only I did stand up to them instead of taking it and pretending like it didn't humiliate me. But I have changed since then. I am stronger, wiser, and I would think, a little more confident." Maddy was right. It was time to take a stand. Angie would let Enrico know exactly how he hurt her before and that she wasn't going to let it happen a second time.

Chapter 11

SCHOOL WOES

Angie savoured the spring breeze as she strolled past a Carlton bookshop. She crossed the road and made her way through Lygon Court while dodging passersby on her way to Brunetti's. Heading through the open doors and into the cafe, Angie's eyes roamed the jam-packed space of patrons eating, conversing, or buying sweets, savouries, and coffee. She walked along the shiny flooring and sat on a seat to wait for Enrico. Her body trembled and her breath quickened. She must've been mentally tired and her body was bearing the brunt of it. She wasn't in the headspace to confront the past, but if she didn't, when would she? It was a gaping hole that would grow the longer she left it. Pondering the past only brought tears, but she refused to weep.

A voice made her move in her seat. "Angie." The smell of spice mixed with citrus drew her in closer.

She dismissed his magnetic presence. "Hello, Enrico."

He grimaced. "Angie."

She rose from the table, thinking she could at least be polite after he apologised. "What would you like? You got the drinks last time so I'll get them this time."

He leaned in close, his white t-shirt pressing against his muscled chest and his jeans fitting him like a second skin. No-one should look that good, especially not the enemy. She had to remember that he was, in fact, the enemy. She couldn't trust him.

"I'll have a strong cappuccino, thanks."

He walked around the table, and she stared at his back; his body looked strong and fit. *Of course he is fit, she scolded herself. He's a police officer.* She returned ten minutes later, carrying a tray of two cappuccinos and a tiramisu.

She settled the tray on the table. "I couldn't resist the sweet. Would you like a bit?" Angie sat down.

"No, you enjoy it."

He rested his back against the chair as they sipped on their coffees. "Now, you're not going to run out on me again, are you?"

She kept her expression neutral. "No, I'm not."

"Glad to hear it." He gave her an awkward grin.

Angie focused on her drink. She could manage polite conversation for now. "So how do you keep yourself busy while you're not working?"

He put down his coffee. "I like to make things out of wood. Just recently, I made a bookshelf."

She frowned. "Right. I should have known. The book you bought."

There was a sudden twinkle in his eye. "As you found out at the meeting, I'm a policeman and don't get much time for hobbies. A sign of the times in my line of work."

She wouldn't have expected him to become a cop, but then again, his need for control did make him suitable. He picked up his coffee and his eyes lingered on his mug. She sipped on her own drink.

"Interesting work. My brother, Jimmy, loves carpentry, too. My stepfather's in the custom woodwork business." Why was she rambling? She shared too much information. Taking a bite of her tiramisu, she savoured the sweet texture and density of the cake. When she looked up, his lips parted as he watched her with interest.

His eyes darkened. "I think we need to talk about things, Angie. Make everything transparent. Don't you think?" He fumbled with his napkin and touched the base of his neck.

Angie's chest tightened. Was she ready for this? But she knew it was inevitable if they were going to keep working together for the next few months. "What? How you bullied me in school or how your stupid friend, Jake pretended to like me, humiliated me in front of everyone, then took a photo of us kissing to prove he won your stupid bet. How is that fair?"

He stared down at the floor then tapped a fist against his lips. "I am sorry about that, but I have changed. Everything we did was wrong and childish. I am not that person anymore. Forgive me?"

She bit her bottom lip. "Forgiveness has to be earned, Enrico, and simple words are empty. How can I trust you when I know you and your friends were just liars and bullies? Gina called me an ice queen just the other day!"

He clenched his hands. "I must admit I was under peer pressure, and I'm not proud for calling you an ice queen or a loser in high school, but you never stood up for yourself. In fact, you showed no emotion." He looked past her briefly. "You didn't show that you cared what we were doing to you. In my mind, I think I wanted to get a reaction from you, but it was an immature way to go about it."

"If I appeared standoffish, it was only a defence mechanism. Inside I was crying like you wouldn't believe. I was a mess, but I had to be strong, and apparently, that makes it seem like I have no emotions. It was the only way I could get through it and everything else I was faced with, and your bullying kept going on for years."

Enrico blinked rapidly, taking another sip of his drink. "I am sorry. Truly. We saw your mother drunk at times, and we judged you for it. We judged you because of the way you dressed and looked because of your braces. We judged you because you seemed to not care, and that made me mad because, like I said, I probably wanted a rise out of you. Hell, we judged you for being poorer than us, and it was shallow. I know that now. But I wish you had retaliated. We deserved it."

She shrugged. "You didn't know my damn story because you didn't want to know. I was finding a way to cope, and I didn't say anything because of my mum. I didn't want to make things worse for her. She had enough to deal with. I didn't want to add to it."

"I can understand that. I was an idiot, but I'm not the same guy."

"So you keep saying." Angie remained silent. There wasn't anything else she could say. She wondered if he had changed. But what he and his friends had done would be hard to truly get over. She needed to process things in her own time. The name calling wasn't even the worst of it. She had allowed herself to be vulnerable with Jake; and they had all violated her vulnerability and trust and had a hand in breaking her heart.

After further awkward silence, Enrico peered at his watch and got up from his chair. "We should get to those venues before they close."

And that was it. It was all out in the open, just as Maddy suggested. Angie wasn't sure it was going to help any, though.

They walked a fair bit of distance from each other, the tension still thick in the air.

Was she ready to forgive Enrico and could she learn to trust him?

Chapter 12

AN AGREEMENT

E nrico exited from Ray's car the following Wednesday night. When they reached the bookshop and rang the doorbell, footsteps sounded inside. Angie swung open the door. Her coldness disappeared; her face glowed in the moonlight. She had a sensual appeal about her Enrico hadn't noticed before. The tight-knit jumper and woollen skirt with stockings she wore displayed her feminine curves.

"Hi, Angie," said Ray. She ignored him. "I am sorry about the past, and I've grown up since then. Time to move on, don't you think?"

Enrico shoved his friend. "Oh, cut it out, Ray. That is rude, and this isn't the damn time." He nodded in her direction. "Angie."

"Enrico." She was rubbing her hand down her right leg as if she was itchy. She scraped her long fingers through her glossy hair.

They entered the room, Angie leading the way, and sat on the couch while she opened the small fridge and carried out the crackers, kabana, and cheese. She hefted the two jugs of water, setting them on the table. Her hands shook and her face reddened, then she answered the door again.

Jenna entered the room. "Hi guys." She wrapped her arms around Angie. "Hey, Angie. Enrico. I'll let the rest of them inside. They're coming now."

The fresh smell of pine filled his senses as Angie wandered over to the couch and sat motionless beside him with her hands clasped together. Their legs brushed and he ignored his quickened breath. He had to focus on earning her trust.

As she came in Gina smirked at Angie. Ray gave Gina a nudge and shook his head as if he was annoyed with her. "Don't be rude," he whispered

"Okay, people. I'm going around the room to report on progress. We'll start with Enrico and Angie. How did you guys go with the catering venues? Any ideas there?"

"Angie and I have been making progress." Enrico ignored the glaring looks from Gina. "We have a few possibilities. I'll show you a few photos of the food and menus on my phone, then I'll talk prices and the type of service. We can do this as a process of elimination, but I've got a few more catering venues we can visit around the city."

He pulled out his phone and passed it around. As the others flipped through the photos, he gawked at Angie's profile. She had slim, tanned legs and he wondered if she worked out. He had started to wonder a lot of things about her, and it bothered him. After his bad run of relationships, he wasn't after anything, but when had she become so damn attractive? He couldn't stop staring at her. This was bad news. They may have aired everything out, but she was right. He and his friends had been horrible to her. If Enrico was in Angie's place, he would be upset and distrustful too. Jenna returned the phone to him.

Jenna made a few notes on a piece of paper and ticked something off. She turned to Enrico and Angie. "Visit a few more places, then we'll pool them together and decide in the next month or two. Now, let's have the marketing team." She turned to Gina and Ray.

Gina straightened her spine. "Given my journalistic profession, I've started the school page, sourcing contacts, and working on a flyer." She rambled on about technical issues but Enrico switched off. Eventually, Susie and Tim gave their spiel about entertainment, discussing the work of a few musicians and DJs.

After making the rounds, Jenna's eyes shone in the bright lighting of the staff room. "I wanted to propose we do something social together. There's a nightclub I've been dying to go to. Are you guys in?"

"I'm in," said Enrico.

"It depends on the date, Jenna. We'll see," said Gina who kept leering at Angie beside him. Why hadn't Gina grown up after all these years?

Jenna intervened. "Let me know who wants to come and I'll text you the details. I'll let you know the date, but we should all try to make it." Taking a breath, she said, "Okay, guys. Why don't we check out Angie's bookshop and the building next door and confirm we're using it as our venue?"

As they strolled over to the empty building next door, Angie rushed up ahead and whispered something to Jenna while Gina took hold of Enrico's arm. He pushed her away and approached Tim who nodded in his direction. "I love the space. We have plenty of room for a DJ and a buffet table, and even a dance section," said Tim.

Jenna smiled. "Exactly right, Tim. And in the back of the bookshop behind the stairs is a good place to keep drinks and other foods. Some people might have a preference to staying here and others in the bookstore."

Tim leaned forward. "We do need to add a DJ table of about six feet and look at audiovisual capabilities." He placed his ring finger across his temple, deep in thought.

Enrico touched Tim on the shoulder. "I'm good with my hands and can easily make a DJ table and even help to set up the audiovisual equipment for the slideshows. We'll also need a buffet table or a coffee bar away from the dance floor."

Tim nodded. "Sounds good, Enrico."

Angie glared at him. "I don't need your help, Enrico. I can get my stepdad to make a couple of those tables. You don't need to worry about that."

He wanted to help, but she was turning him down. Not that he blamed her, but he needed to show her he was no longer that bad guy. She was making it difficult. "I don't mind. I love doing woodwork and I'm good at it."

Tim moved towards Angie. "Let him do it. He can work straight inside this building instead of having to transport the tables here from his place."

She took a moment to process it and sighed. Angie knew there was a limited budget within the committee. She hated to rely on her stepfather when he was currently busy trying to drum up more business for his work. So she could use all the help she could get. "Fine."

"I assume you all approve of this venue if Enrico's putting his carpentry skills to use?" Everyone except Gina put up their hands. "Gina?" Jenna asked.

She nodded. "I guess it'll do." She avoided Angie's eyes.

They made their way over to the bookshop, and as he took a step into it, he was in awe of the size of the store featuring shelves upon shelves of books with a huge space for the counter, filled with book accessories and more books. He hadn't got a clear look of the shop the last time he came when his mind had been on Angie.

The group returned to the staffroom, where everyone made notes and Angie made a rough plan of how to arrange the rooms for the venue.

Jenna rose. "Okay, guys. That's it for tonight. I will see you at our big night out and text you the details."

Enrico stood up and beamed at Angie who was silent. She hurried to the door to usher them all out, and waved goodbye to everyone except for Gina and Ray. Enrico stayed behind. He wanted to talk to her again. "Wait at the car," he said to Ray. "I'll be a minute." His friend nodded and left.

Enrico stood awkwardly opposite Angie with his hands in his pockets. "I think you're doing a great thing, giving us this room to meet, and for having your place of business as our venue."

"Given that you wanted to replace my venue with another one, I don't know what to say." She huffed. "Listen, I'm tired and I think you should go." He was trying here, but she refused him point-blank. Why couldn't she meet him halfway? He hated how aloof and controlled she was.

"Alright. Have a good night." He let himself out and caught up with Ray.

She still hated him, and he hated himself, too.

Chapter 13

JEALOUSY

A few days later, Enrico parked his car on the side of the road across from Angie's bookshop. He had to make this right, and he hoped he was doing the right thing. Bullying her had been wrong, but he'd been angry at the world when his father died. There was Angie acting aloof and emotionless, and he had been triggered. Jealous that nothing seemed to affect her, hurt her. But he had been wrong. She had been hurting, and he had caused her pain. His heart ached at the idea of Angie hurting because of him. He had been such a childish fool. He wasn't a child nor a fool now. He would show her that.

Enrico gripped his wallet and walked along the busy shopping strip, his back slightly aching from an altercation with a criminal earlier in the week. The cold chilled him to the bone.

When her shop came into view, he froze. She hadn't asked him here. She made it clear that she wanted nothing to do with him. If Enrico showed up out of the blue, what would she think of him? He was about to turn back when he spotted Angie disappearing into her bookshop a few stores down; thankfully, she didn't see him. He could drop in, purchase a book, and leave quickly. He'd be supporting her business, and they could start to put the past behind them. It was a better reason than trying to apologise again. He'd be acknowledging her hard work and success after all these years. If conversation and situation allowed, he could try to plead his case.

He browsed the promotional posters around the store, which made the place striking and visible with its three-dimensional book images of a thriller box set fiction release by an author whose name he couldn't pronounce. Other posters promoted spiritual and health non-fiction books, as well as an upcoming book signing by a local author he'd never heard of.

The downlights gave the store a relaxed ambience. Several customers lazily explored the literary labyrinth, and a good few were lined up to pay. Maddy was serving customers at the till. Angie was on a stepladder, filling the upper part of a bookshelf with thick books. The movements she made—nestling the stack of books on her hip, stretching out her arm to place a book on a shelf—accentuated the feminine curves of her body. He focused in a different direction, not wanting to leer like a creep. She was busy. Maybe he shouldn't have come.

He stepped onto thick blue carpeting and perused the new releases bookshelf. He loved thrillers, so he retrieved a hardcover book. The book had a fresh scent with its crisp, cream pages, and the blurb intrigued him. Flicking through the pages, Enrico found himself unable to focus on its contents. His heart beat fast and his mouth felt dry. What was he nervous about? He had every right to buy a book; that was why he was here. It had nothing to do with how often he found himself thinking about Angie, wanting to see her again. Nothing to do with the guilt he felt at having hurt her. He was here to buy a book and support a local business.

"Enrico. Why are you here?"

He snapped the book shut a bit too forcefully and turned to face her. He took a breath, his mind fuzzy at the way she scanned him from head to foot, taking him in. She wore a tight-fitted red t-shirt showing her toned upper torso and blue ripped jeans, displaying sensual curves. *Oh, god. Get it together, man!* "Hi Angie. I'm sorry to drop in like this, but I...I...was curious and needed to get a particular book."

She put her hands on her hips, her eyes gleaming in the light. "Right." She faked a smile. "Do you need help with anything?" Her mouth tightened.

He shouldn't have come. He had crossed into her territory unwanted, and that was clear from the way she forced a smile that didn't reach her eyes. She still hated him. Her hate cut him to the core.

"Enrico. It's been a long time," said Maddy.

Startled, Enrico took a step back from Angie. He clenched the book in his hand, his mind on Angie's glowering eyes. "Hi, Maddy. It's good to see you again."

Angie moved off. "I have to go, but feel free to browse, Enrico." She stormed off like an express train. She couldn't get away fast enough. He stood there opposite Maddy. Her professional smile took on an edge of coldness.

"I hope you have changed Enrico, or you'll be dealing with me." Maddy wandered off and approached the counter while Angie served another customer in the non-fiction section.

He calmed his fast breathing and headed to the area of books on woodwork and fitness close by. He picked up a book which had a chapter on advanced wood carving techniques.

Enrico headed to the new releases table and picked up two thriller novels he'd skimmed through earlier, waiting for Angie to head to the counter. When she made her way over, he approached her, but as he grew near she clenched her jaw and drew her shoulders back with irritation.

"I'll take these," he said softly, trying to keep the guilt out of his voice.

She put the books into a recyclable cloth bag. "Good choice. Exactly what I would've chosen. I like thrillers, too."

"Really?" He felt his eyebrows rise and heard the excitement driving his voice a little too high. He cleared his throat and she looked at him with confusion.

Angie scanned the books into her till. "Cash or card?"

"Credit," he said as he eventually swiped his card. Her fingers brushed against his as she handed him a receipt and his books, sending warmth up his arm.

He nodded and focused on two other customers waiting in line behind him. "I'll give you a call about the next venue visits."

"Fine." She clasped her hands at her side.

He could take a hint.

He walked out of the store and let out a breath of frustration. He may not be a child anymore, but he was definitely still a fool. Once he reached a cafe for a much-needed coffee a few stores down, he shook his head at himself for invading her space. She was uncomfortable, and he moved too quickly before she was ready to forgive him fully. He turned back to glance at the bookshop across the street. He stopped short at the sight of two people standing outside Angie's shop. One of them was a handsome, solidly built man with wavy, brown hair who had his arms around Angie. They pulled apart and she kissed him on his forehead. The way they stood close together made him brim with envy.

Enrico snatched up his coffee off the counter, hissing as the hot liquid splashed against his skin. He transferred the to-go cup to his other hand and shook off the liquid, wiping the remainder off on his pant leg. She had a boyfriend. An older man. Not that he cared. She was free to see whoever she liked, and it wasn't his concern. He had no right to harbour feelings of jealousy. They were just acquaintances working on their high school reunion together. Nothing more. Angie clearly hoped for less from him. He climbed into the driver's seat of his car and put the hot cup into the holder beside him. He was a fool, and if he kept being a fool he would never get Angie's forgiveness. Enrico pulled out into traffic and drove home.

Chapter 14

NIGHT-CLUBBING

Two weeks later, Enrico was sitting at the dinner table with his family. "Earth to Enrico. Earth to Enrico. What's up with you tonight? Your bolognaise is getting cold," said his mother.

He picked at his food, having lost his appetite lately. "Nothing, Mum." He twirled a strand of spaghetti onto his fork and shoved it in his mouth, not tasting anything. He had to please his mother when it came to food, or she'd have his hide.

"He's in lust, Mum," said Stella, who glanced at her mother and got her frowning.

Enrico glared at Stella. "What are you talking about?"

"The school reunion. I knew you'd take a liking to Angie. The way you've spoken about your so-called mission together. Anyone with half a brain would know you like the girl. But isn't she a bit too smart for you, brother?"

His mind ruminated on the truth of her words. Did he like Angie that way or was he just trying to make amends? Once they finished up with the reunion, he would probably never see her again. "Funny, aren't you? But no. I do not like Angie. She is interesting and we talked about the past, but we are acquaintances, that is all. She also hates me and I don't blame her." He hated to admit that fact.

Stella held her fork in the air. "Hmm. Whatever you say, bro."

His mother scrutinised him over her drink. "What is it between you two, Enrico?"

Oh, Christ! What had Stella started? He made small, jittery movements with his fingers, his pulse quickening. "She's fine now. No more issues, so can we leave the past in the past, Mum?"

His mother clutched at his arm. "I demand to know what's going on, Enrico."

His mother didn't know how he had bullied her, but eventually he would need to tell her.

"You need to tell Mum the truth, bro." She was right. His mother wouldn't let this go.

"I will tell you another time, Mum."

His mother buried herself into her food without even looking at him "Fine, son. I will hold you to that."

Enrico smiled reassuringly at his mother then finished his bolognaise. "I'm going out tonight. Don't wait up." He was meeting the group from the committee at a nightclub.

His mother leaned in. "Where are you going, and who with? Ray and Lorenzo?"

"I'm socialising at a nightclub with the reunion committee. Ray will be there, yes." He rose from the table, put his dishes in the sink and picked up his car keys. He would soon find out if he'd see Angie again.

Climbing down three steps, Angie glanced at the green, pink, and purple hues in the nightclub, the lights and shadows reflecting on the shiny square flooring. A bar featuring an elongated counter with a multitude of stools stood alongside the dance floor. The dark, romantic ambience suited the current ballad playing over the speakers. Women and men dressed to impress filled the area. The ceilings were replete with lined patterns and strobe lights.

She almost hadn't come tonight and mentioned to Jenna she would not attend, but after Jenna explained how Enrico was trying to please her and had changed over the years, she thought she'd at least go for Jenna's sake.

Angie waved to Enrico, who was sitting at a table near the bar holding a thick glass. He was seated alongside Jenna and Ray. She couldn't help but appreciate his outfit—black satin shirt, white pants, and brown Italian leather shoes. He drew his muscular hand across his fringe then set down his glass and waved back, as did Ray and Jenna.

"You look amazing," said Jenna.

Angie wore an above the knee-length white dress, fitting snugly around her waist to show her slim curves. Black wedges and a black wrap-around shawl complimented the dress.

"Thanks, Jenna. I love your dress."

Jenna wore a tight, red cotton dress belted around the waist underneath a short black cardigan. She chuckled. "Oh, this old thing. It's from a second-hand shop but I've made good use of it."

She seated herself between Jenna and Enrico. "So Susie and Tim couldn't make it?"

"No, they had other plans tonight. It's just the four of us. Gina couldn't come either." Enrico's eyes lingered in her direction as she pressed on her bottom lip, sitting awkwardly while gripping the strap of her black clutch. Her heart raced, and the back of her neck sweated. Jenna and Ray conversed among themselves.

"What would you like to drink? My shout." Enrico asked.

Ray intervened. "I can get you a drink, Angie. It's the least I can do after all that school crap, you know. Like I said before, I have matured since then."

The scent of musk and spices permeated her senses. The curve of Enrico's lip brought a tingle to her chest. She wondered what he was really like, and couldn't help noticing that his lips looked soft and his hands strong. His dark eyes held a tinge of sadness. She pushed those thoughts aside, still sceptical of Enrico and Ray. "I'll have a dry house red."

Jenna faced Ray. "I'll help you with the drinks." *No, don't leave me with Enrico.* Angie's eyes pleaded with Jenna but she didn't seem to catch on. Jenna and Ray walked to the bar, leaving the two of them alone. Angie and Enrico remained silent, both staring out at the crowd.

Enrico cleared his throat.

The lingering smells of perfumes, residual smoke, and colognes filled the room, and the muffled voices blended in well with the thump of the rap music. "So how's the bookshop business going?" He had a hint of a smile.

Angie drummed her fingers on the table in time to the beat of the music. His body in close proximity made her quiver. "Fine for now." She turned away when Jenna and Ray returned with a tray of drinks. She picked up her wine and drank most of it down. It soothed her dry throat and helped to numb her jittery fingers. She engaged in small talk with Jenna while Enrico snuck glances in her direction. It was going to be a long night.

Angie didn't want to focus on him tonight. She could easily enjoy her time with Jenna who had always been nice to her. She would wait until Jenna left and leave at the same time. No need to stick around if it was only her and Enrico. She would be sick at the thought.

Chapter 15

RESCUE

Angie clasped her hands several drinks later when Jenna stood up. "I'm beat so I'm going home." She hugged Angie and waved to Enrico and Ray.

"Thanks for the great night, Jenna. We'll see you soon," said Angie.

Ray scanned the remainder of the crowd. "Bye, guys. I'm off too. Duty calls." He focused on Enrico. "I'll see you at the station on Monday, bro."

"Sure, Ray. See you then," said Enrico.

A few minutes later, Angie rose. "I'm going, too."

Enrico knit his brows, reaching out to her but stopping in mid-process. He seemed disappointed but she had to be misreading him. "No, don't go. Have another drink. We can go where it's more private. You and I really need to talk and we can't do it here."

Angie shook her head. "I thought we already did that. Talking can be over-rated."

He leaned forward. "I want you to understand who I am today and not back then. You still hate me. I can tell," Enrico said.

She sighed heavily. "What the hell do you expect? You can't honestly think I am suddenly okay with the past. You cannot magically click your fingers, and I will trust you again. We have a job to do, so let's just focus on that." Was he attempting to make up for the past, or did he want to make himself feel better? They hadn't fully resolved everything, but was it even worth it?

"I'm going to the ladies' room then I'll leave." She headed in that direction, thinking how Enrico's softened expression earlier touched something in her. But no, he was still a jerk underneath.

Enrico peered at his mobile phone, wondering why Angie refused to give him a chance. She didn't want to try to understand him, but he knew it would take time, and he was a patient man. He wondered if he could intervene after she came out of the bathroom, to convince her to stay and have another drink. Or did that seem a little too pushy? He didn't want to be too controlling, as that could show in her mind that he was still a bully. Her vibrant green eyes and full lips were etched into his brain like they were carved permanently into stone. He was thinking about her a lot, which was crazy when they barely knew each other.

A few minutes later, Angie walked out of the ladies' room and made her way towards the exit. Their eyes locked but she quickly looked away and rushed her way forward.

Enrico eyed a drunk man coming in her direction and he made his way towards her.

"Come on, one dance, gorgeous. I'll show you a good time." The man grasped her by the shoulder. Angie shoved him away. "Leave me alone." He clutched her arm. He swayed and ended up knocking into

Angie whose body and face fell forward into Enrico's arms. Her breath hitched while his throat was parched and his vocal cords frozen. Their eyes lingered as he held her around the small of her back. His body craved more of her touch. Why did it bother him so much that the feel of Angie's body made him warm and fuzzy inside?

The drunk man broke into the moment. "Come on, love. Just one dance." Angie scowled at the man and shoved him away, but he wouldn't budge.

Enrico made a beeline towards him. "Let her go or you'll have me to deal with." He glared. "I am a police officer, and I can have you in a cell before you can say help." The man scoffed and walked away. He turned to Angie. "Are you alright?

"I'm fine." She stood awkwardly and gripped the straps of her bag.

"Let me walk you to your car. I'm leaving too."

She walked ahead of him. "Whatever."

As they moved in a strange silence, he let her get into her car, ensuring she was safe, not wanting to pressure her with further discussion. "I'll be seeing you, Angie," said Enrico.

Angie rolled down her window. "Goodbye." She waved to him with a neutral expression, started the car, and drove off.

Chapter 16

POLICE WORK

E nrico walked into the brown and grey brick police building on Monday, swinging open the door. The buzz of activity spiked his adrenaline as he waved and greeted his fellow policemen. He walked through to the staffroom and poured himself a coffee. He took a sip, his mind turning back to his night with Angie, who had shown annoyance at their close encounter at the club. She had flown out of the club quicker than a fighter jet, and in spite of walking her to her car, he couldn't stop her from driving off so fast. But when that man had harassed her, it had made him think how he had behaved in a similar way all those years ago. In spite of their connection, now, Angie held back as if she didn't want to forgive him for the past? Would she ever?

He was jerked out of his reverie when voices sounded behind him. Ray and Lorenzo both clapped him on the back. "Great to see you, mate," said Ray.

Ray fiddled with the espresso machine and shook his head. Enrico knew he'd never made his own coffee, always bribing the administrative assistant to make one for him. He'd soon have to learn.

Lorenzo chortled, shaking his head. "As you can see, nothing's changed with the machine. Ray's still hopeless with it."

"He sure is," said Enrico.

Ray stepped back and let Lorenzo take over with the machine. "How was it with Angie last night? Did you get any alone time?"

The noise of the espresso machine drowned out any possible answer. Enrico's eyes roamed the room, scanning the special notices, poster displays of 'coffee with a cop,' awards for bravery by a majority of the police force, and news stories of the latest misdemeanours and serious crimes.

The machine quieted and Lorenzo handed Ray a cup. He sipped his coffee. "You didn't answer my question about Angie."

Enrico shrugged. "She left not long after you did and still hates me. I walked her to her car after a man was being a creep and trying to force her to dance, then went home."

Ray sat at the table opposite Lorenzo. It occurred to Enrico that Lorenzo had little idea who they were talking about since he hadn't attended their school. He gave a quick accounting of Angie and their history to catch Lorenzo up.

"She seems to have warmed up a bit. I mean, the first time we saw her at the meeting, she was cold and angry towards us. Last night, she was less icy towards you. Give it time, mate. But I think she's hot for you. I can see it," Ray said.

Enrico's skin warmed. "That's ridiculous."

"Whatever you say, man," said Ray. He eyed Lorenzo and explained the situation.

Enrico changed the subject. "What's on for today?"

"We've got reports of drag racers close to the city suburbs, so I'm checking it out today, questioning any witnesses, locating home surveillance cameras, and returning to those residences if they're not home in the day. You're welcome to join," said Lorenzo.

Enrico nodded. "Sounds interesting, but the Sergeant wants me doing other work. He said we have new recruits he wants me to oversee."

Ray nodded. "I'm joining Lorenzo on the drag racing trail if you don't want the responsibility."

Enrico shook his head. "I love those opportunities when I can train the Newbies on patrol. The Sergeant did give me the choice but he knows I enjoy mentoring." The men walked out of the room and headed to a meeting before Enrico paired up with a police constable, new on the job.

In the conference room, the administrative assistant gave out a tray of sweets. She got the officers together to welcome the new recruits by passing around pieces of cake before they all headed out for the day's duties. He sank his teeth into a chocolate liquid which dripped down his chin and wiped it with a napkin. Turning to his fellow police officer, he nodded. "Ready for the streets?"

The new police officer, Constable Peter Jonesy, a tall, lanky man with stubble around his chin and a wild demeanour, grinned. "As ready as can be, Senior Constable Enrico Delluci."

"Please call me Enrico. No need to be so formal."

"Certainly, sir."

They made their way into the police car in the nearby garage, and Enrico drove down the streets of Coburg. He took hold of the speaker. "Copy that. We'll follow it up." He turned to Peter. "Okay, Constable, are you up for a speeding driver on Albion Street?"

"Yes, sir. We're not far from there. Approximately five minutes."

Enrico turned on his siren and headed towards the incident. "It appears the driver allegedly cut people off and might be drug or alcohol affected."

"I look forward to the experience, Senior Constable Delluci."

He turned towards the policeman who looked excited, willing and eager. "As I said before, please call me Enrico."

"Copy, that, Senior Cons—I mean Enrico."

Once they reached the small car zigzagging its way down the busy road, the female driver eventually stopped with the policemen on her tail.

It was going to be a long day.

Chapter 17

CHANCE ENCOUNTER

E nrico jumped into his black SUV and drove towards the Carlton pub. He was tired of being in the middle of his mother's rants about his high school days after he explained his bullying ways. Did she not know how sorry he was for the past? He learned from it now, but he couldn't change that fact.

A car horn beeped behind him when he slowed down, having reached Cardigan Street in Carlton. He put on his blinker and parked in the street then walked outside with a view of the University of Melbourne up ahead. As he neared the pub, his mind focused on Angie, who he wanted to ring. Several times he was about to click on her number, but his fingers froze. He wasn't sure why he wanted to ring her.

Pushing aside an image of her, he entered the pub, skirted around the high timber tables and square chairs, then headed towards his friends, Ray and Lorenzo who were already holding beers.

"Hey guys. Sorry, I'm late."

"No worries, mate," said Ray. "No girls here yet, but the night's still young."

Enrico shook his head. "Is that all you think about?"

Ray angled his head. "Hey, I'm free and single and so are you."

Lorenzo drew a hand across his long, curly shoulder-length hair, tied up in a low ponytail. "Enrico likes Angie. Jenna came over with her husband the other day and spoke about how great it was to see her again."

Enrico sat around the table opposite them. "I do not like Angie, okay? I don't even know her all that well." He got up and ordered a beer from the counter.

The tables slowly filled up, with several customers sitting outside in a beer garden noticeable through an open window. It was starting to get loud with voices, the clinking of glasses, and trays of food and nibbles. He took a handful of beer nuts from a tray in the centre of the table and wondered if Angie would like this place. *Stop it!* he scolded himself.

"Anyway, mate. Tell us again why you won't ask her out already. She might hate you, but there's a part of her that seems dead keen to me." Ray watched him with concern.

He avoided his eyes. "I think she has a boyfriend and I don't want to get in the way."

Lorenzo turned to Ray and they shared a strange look. "Listen, mate. I know Gina did a number on you back in high school, but it's been years. They're not all cheaters like Gina."

"Easy for you to say. You're married with three children. Besides, I thought Gina was special at the time, but I'm over it. She's old news."

"If you're not sure whether she has a boyfriend or not, shouldn't you be asking her?" Lorenzo said.

Enrico swallowed. "It's none of my business, Lorenzo. And like I told you, we're working together on this school reunion. Nothing more." He wanted to explain how close they came to kissing at the nightclub, but he wouldn't live it down with them.

Ray gripped his beer. "If you say so. Whatever lies you want to tell yourself, bro."

Lorenzo faced the door, appearing momentarily distracted. "Anyone with eyes can see you like the girl. I know you still have the past to settle but set her straight, Enrico. Then later tell her how you feel." Ray suddenly made a low whistle.

"What are you looking at?" Enrico followed his friends' line of sight towards the entrance. *Angie!* He jerked upright and straightened his hair before he could stop himself.

Ray slid in his seat. "That woman with Angie is hot. But they're with a guy."

He turned to his side, and sure enough, right in his view was Angie with the guy and her friend, Maddy. It was the same man she had kissed outside her shop.

Angie was positively radiant in her silky pink singlet top and tight-fitting black jeans that clung to her slim, toned legs. She walked in with an air of sweetness, and he imagined what her lips would taste like. He imagined what it would be like to hold her tightly and never let her go. The alcohol was getting to him already; he wasn't thinking straight.

Angie walked into the crowded pub with Maddy and Gerard, and her breath caught when she spotted Enrico. He was sitting with two other men gawking in their direction as they sat by the bar. She waved to Enrico who smiled and waved back. He focused hard on Gerard who sat beside her. Maddy sat opposite them.

She eyed Maddy. "What do I do? Enrico's here."

Maddy briefly turned to Gerard then back at Angie. "Go and talk to him."

Gerard knit his brows. "Who are we talking about?" He gazed towards the male group. "Are you talking about the group of testosterone over there?"

Maddy laughed but Angie glanced into her lap, her heart hammering against her chest. Her whole body shook as she wondered why Enrico wouldn't come to her. "Yes, two of the men went to my school."

Gerard nodded. "Oh, that's Enrico who you've been working with?" He pressed his lips together. "The guy cannot take his eyes off you, Angie."

They had all gone out for pizza earlier. Why had they come to this pub afterwards? If she'd known Enrico would be here, she would've gone back home.

"Listen, go to the bar and order drinks. He should talk to you then. He must be intimidated by the group." Maddy turned to Gerard and explained the situation.

"I don't trust the guy, Maddy. We're not even friends."

Maddy squinted. "I caught him staring at you at school sometimes. I think even then he liked you, but was too gutless to say anything. Maybe it was a combination of peer pressure and stupidity, and he was a creep. You have to lay things on the table. Be honest about how he made you feel. Now's your chance."

"I did that already," Angie said. "It hasn't changed anything, Maddy." She was only protecting herself. Maybe she needed to give him the chance to prove that he had changed. She relented. "Fine. I'll go and buy us drinks, but not so Enrico can talk to me. I'm just thirsty." She got up from her chair and didn't dare look over at Enrico and his friends. She hovered at the countertop, fighting against a dry mouth and quivering, twitchy muscles in her stomach. "I'll have a beer and two sweet martinis, please."

The burly bartender nodded. "Coming right up."

Her legs became unsteady, so she supported her body against the countertop and waited for the bartender to pour the martini into the glasses. He worked on the next concoction and gave her a brief smile while he poured and mixed the drinks. She waited, counting down the seconds but no sign of Enrico. Why did she care that he didn't come talk to her when she didn't know whether she could trust him? It was probably best they keep to themselves. But a part of her thought back to the club and how their bodies had pressed closely together. She pondered how he had helped her with that creepy, drunk guy pushing her to dance, but that could have just been a show.

When the bartender finished up their drinks, she paid in cash and gathered them up on a tray. The familiar scent of musk penetrated her nose. Turning, she smiled at an awkward Enrico, whose eyes filled with doubt. "So how have you been, Angie?"

She moved closer. "Fine, thanks. And you?"

"Good. I've been busy at work."

"That's good. Busy is good." Over his shoulder, she could see his friends watching. Uneasiness settled in her chest. She couldn't help but remember a similar scene when Enrico had been among his friends, watching as Jake broke up with her and revealed that he was only with her because of a bet.

That was a long time ago, she reminded herself. She glanced down, wishing her hands weren't full so she could sip her drink and ease her nerves a bit. When she looked back up, Enrico eyes still lingered. Why wouldn't he say something?

Enrico gestured with his eyes. "So who's the guy?"

"He's a friend. That neighbour I mentioned."

His eyes shone. "Right." He tapped his fingers against the counter-top. "Listen, why don't you and your friends join us at our table?"

Her chest tightened. Maybe this wasn't the right place to make small conversation with him. "I don't think so."

He hid his disappointment. "No worries."

She walked off and explained to her friends what Enrico had suggested.

Maddy shook her head. "Oh, come on, Angie. I think the guy's trying here. Maybe he has changed. Give him a chance to show you."

Before she had a chance to respond, Ray approached, nodding to others and turning to Angie. "Listen, Angie. I know we were jerks, but Enrico and I are different now. Call it maturity, wisdom, and heartache over the years, but we have changed. Get to know us." His expression softened. "Can we please join you?"

Gerard intervened. "One drink, Angie, and then we'll leave."

Angie was overwhelmed and gave in. "Fine. Come on over."

As they joined tables and settled into the group, Enrico scrutinised Gerard. He had no right to be jealous when he held no claim on her. Not that she cared anyway.

While Maddy, Ray, and Lorenzo spoke amongst themselves, Gerard looked Enrico straight in the eye. "Angie and I are just friends. She's like the sister I never had."

Angie slumped her shoulders and gritted her teeth, shooting Gerard a look. Her friends were making things awkward.

Enrico's eyes lit up as he eyed Angie, appearing relaxed and casual for the remainder of the night. "Good to know, Gerard."

Angie's chest tightened. She couldn't let him get the upper hand here. She was nowhere near close to forgiving him.

Later in the night, Enrico bought them a round of drinks and the group talked about the latest thriller movies they enjoyed. She observed how Enrico suddenly got quiet, and how his eyes drew away as if in deep thought. Angie wondered what he was thinking.

He leaned in towards her with his hands fidgeting while others spoke amongst themselves. "How about dinner next Friday night at the Docklands?"

Angie couldn't help but feel a flutter in her stomach and wondered whether she heard him right. "Excuse me?"

His face turned red. "I mean, it's purely reunion committee business. This restaurant is owned by another friend, and he offers catering for events too. They come well-recommended. It's the last one and then we'll decide on the caterer."

She sighed with relief. "Oh, if it's the last caterer, sure. I guess so."

Chapter 18

DOUBT

A week after the pub, Angie met with Enrico in the city. The local and tourist crowds at the Docklands surrounded them as she savoured the views. She glanced over the waterfront, fixing her gaze on the Melbourne Star Observation Wheel. She walked alongside Enrico. Together, they passed the sports and entertainment centre, a variety of shops and cafes, and the Docklands shopping mall.

They stopped to peer over at the city skyline across Victoria Harbour. Victoria had a lot to offer by way of modernisation and aesthetic appeal. Calmness took over Angie as the night lights beautifully reflected on the rippling water and the distant harbour. She wouldn't want to live anywhere else.

Enrico remained quiet as they took in the view of the surrounding area. He turned to her, looking at her with intensity in his gaze. The wind softly feathered his hair and brought a sweet blush across his square jaw and full lips. "So what did you think of the food? Is it an option for the school reunion?"

She brushed off a flutter in her stomach. "We should certainly consider the docklands catering service for the reunion. It's the best food so far."

Enrico nodded. "I agree. We can let Jenna know and consider booking the catering company. My friend will be excited about it." The warm night led them towards an ice-cream shop where Enrico bought Angie a Zabaglione ice-cream in a cone and a Tiramisu cone for himself. "We still need to talk, Angie. About high school and the way I treated you."

She had dreaded this moment. She held back the tears, thinking back to those times when Gina and her friends had called her an ice queen, an ugly nerd, a loser, the alcoholic daughter, trailer-trash, and the words kept on going. Not to mention the time Enrico's friend, Jake, pretended to like her, kissed her, and took a photo of the kiss, manipulating it into a photo of them having sex in his bed when they never had. He had manipulated other photos of her, too. "I must admit I was shy and lacked confidence because my mum was too busy drinking to be focused on me. But those fake versions of me were sickening."

"I'm sorry we did that, putting your head over a lingerie model's body and the bedroom scene. I should have stopped it."

She scoffed at the image. "What about the naked fake photo of me and the whole class pointing fingers at my assumed disgusting behaviour? Oh, and don't forget the time Gina read my journal to the students in the cafeteria. Or your name-calling, or the time you poured a bucket of sand over my body, which almost blinded me. My eyes hurt for days." Angie shook her head. "I have lost count of the multiple times you and your friends hurt me, humiliated me, and made me feel like dirt. I didn't appreciate you calling me a loser, or trailer trash, or the girl with no prospects. Oh, and did you forget the time you called me Ugly Angie? You even said I wouldn't accomplish much in life. Well, thanks a lot, Enrico."

Enrico bowed his head, playing with the tips of his fingers as if processing what she said. He had no come-back from that. He couldn't change it now, but the explosion in her chest made her want to punch him. It took all her energy not to give him choice words, but she had more dignity than he had ever had.

"I have no real excuse for what I did, and this is not an excuse, Angie. But my father died in my senior year, and I was so angry with the world and with life. I had issues with my mother at the time too, and I felt you hated me even before I bullied you."

She chuckled. "Right. So like you said, you wanted a reaction out of me? Because I didn't like you, you thought you'd take control and humiliate me. Is that it? Great strategy."

"I don't know, Angie. But when you're seventeen, you're stupid and have a lot of growing up to do. I lacked the emotional maturity to get to know you instead of judging you because of your aloofness or the clothes you wore. I could see something else underneath, but I was scared to find out what that was. I am so sorry."

She averted her eyes. "You said sorry already, but it doesn't change anything."

She pulled away and stepped back. She didn't need his pity. "I am stronger because of it. I am no longer the shy, nerdy girl who couldn't assert herself. I've grown since then, and I have yet to decide whether you've grown too."

His posture slouched. "You are your own person and do not need to define yourself by us bullies. I don't keep in touch with them anymore, except for Ray, but he's changed, and I hope you can tell."

Angie wasn't ready for this. Could she trust him completely? Too soon to know. "I'm going home now, Enrico. Thanks for the dinner and ice cream."

She walked away, having had enough memories for one night.

Chapter 19

COFFEE WITH A COP

Enrico's mother gestured with her hand. "So you're off to the city for the coffee with a cop in the shopping centre? It's great to have an event like that."

"Yes. We're talking to the community about local problems and getting to know the public without dealing with crisis all the time. It's about increasing community engagement, and it works well." He had talked to Angie on the phone on Sunday about potentially visiting him at the event, but she said she most likely wouldn't be able to make it. He tried to sell it by getting him to market her bookstore with her business cards, but she was still ambivalent about attending. Not that he blamed her.

His mother moved forward and wrapped her arms around him, but his body stiffened. "I am proud of you, son, and what you've achieved. And I'm sure your father would be proud wherever he is. God bless him."

He smiled awkwardly and pulled away from her. He didn't have time to go down memory lane right this second. He had to be in the right headspace for this public discussion. "Where's Stella?"

"She had an early class this morning."

"What are you up to today?"

She put her cup in the sink. "I might visit Nunziata down the road or my church friend, Sofia. Too many friends and not enough time." His mother peered at her watch. "You better go. It is at ten o'clock this morning, isn't it?"

He grimaced. "Since when did you want me leaving the house?" His eyes roamed. "You don't have a lover stashed here somewhere, do you?"

His mother scoffed. "As if I could ever replace your father. Have a great day."

He nodded. "Okay, I'll see you tonight. Don't get up to mischief."

She started washing the dishes. "Bye, darling." She turned back around. "Please sort out things with Angie. She had a hard life with her mother, not to mention you making it worse as a bully. I know you've atoned for your sins, but you need to make it right with Angie."

"You're right, Mum, and I will." He exited the house and stepped into his car, driving to the city for the much-awaited community engagement program. His mind focused on Angie and the way he was becoming more attached each day. He wanted to make her understand he was truly sorry, but so far, he wasn't getting through to her.

Enrico drove for twenty minutes and swung into a parking space. Walking into the Barkly Square Shopping Centre, he greeted Peter, Lorenzo, and Ray who stood around holding plastic cups of coffee. The stocky owner of the coffee store smiled, headed inside, and returned to bring him a take-away coffee. "Thanks, Burt. You're a life-saver." He turned to his friends and colleagues. "So are we ready for this?"

Lorenzo nodded. "Ray's making a public speech and we'll mingle soon after."

Ray straightened his posture. "I so am. Love the limelight, guys." He walked off to greet a fellow colleague and bumped fists with him.

Peter fixed his gaze curiously on his boss. "Some woman came by asking for you. She said she'll be back shortly, but she rushed off before I could get her name." He frowned. "She was very attractive and might be browsing around the centre."

It must've been Angie. A lightness in his chest and fast pulse led him to bounce from foot to foot. She had to have changed her mind, even if it was about her business.

With a wide grin he watched Ray give an articulate speech about the informal structure of the day, mentioning how the police officers were present for the public to get to know and ask questions of. Who would've thought Ray could be so formal? He was normally so rough with his words, using every opportunity to use idioms and casual language.

Enrico strolled through the centre and stopped by a group who called him over. A woman with coiffed hair and a stiff posture leaned in close. "I want to know what you gentlemen are doing about the high rate of harassment and family violence. I don't believe the cops are doing enough to stop the violence from escalating."

He smiled. "I hear you. What's your name?"

"Judy. So how do policemen deal with it?"

"I appreciate your concerns, and I can assure you we take it very seriously. Firstly, we assess the risk and take into account past family violence and any criminal background. We home in on who is being harmed and who the aggressor is. We ensure everyone in the family is safe and check to see if anyone requires medical attention. If required, we make referrals for each family member and will arrest anyone who is a risk to the family. Believe me. We attempt to stop the situation from escalating. We have progressed in that area."

"It sounds reasonable. Law enforcement has come a long way since the times domestic violence was viewed as a personal matter," Judy said. "Now, what about harassment in the workplace?"

Enrico gave her another spiel, then made his way around the group that gathered. He answered questions, passed around coffee, and gave further spiels about community safety and services. A few other officers took selfies with a group of teenagers.

A familiar voice drew him around. "Hi, Officers. I'm Angie." She shook hands with Peter and Lorenzo while watching Enrico with a hint of a smile. Was she slowly warming up to him? He was about to approach her when a voice rang out. "Excuse me? Officer Dellucci?" It was that woman, Judy, he met earlier. She must have more questions. He made his way over. He hoped that Judy would be quick with her question. Otherwise, Angie might leave as she had taken time off work to be here.

He smiled at Judy and leaned in. "Do you have another question, Judy?"

The woman's eyes shone. "Oh, you remembered my name." She peered past him. "Okay, my question is about the possibility of shadowing a police officer on his day of duties. I would love..." The woman clutched at her chest, closed her eyes, and her body fell forward. He quickly caught her as she struggled to breathe. He turned to a fellow officer. "Call 000. Now." He placed her on the floor with her knees bent while he held her from behind, supporting her head and shoulders. She went limp.

He held tight on the woman and saw her face turning blue. "No, no, no." He checked her pulse. Nothing. Without thought, he lay her flat on the ground and checked her airways. She stopped breathing. He put his mouth over hers to resuscitate her and alternated it with chest compressions. She would not die on his watch. She couldn't die.

Crowds grew around him while other police officers stood around and pushed away the people, getting them to give him space. The woman took a shaky breath, then seemed to continue breathing on her own, though she didn't rouse. He checked her pulse again. It wasn't where it should be, but at least she had a pulse. He let out a sigh of relief. Every few seconds he continued to monitor her.

When the ambulance finally arrived, a tall male paramedic brought out a stretcher with a stout female paramedic. The tall one asked, "What happened? Is she breathing?"

Enrico nodded. "I believe it was a heart attack. I did CPR and she's breathing now."

"Great job, Officer. She should be fine. We'll take her to the Royal Melbourne Hospital." He watched as they checked her vitals, placed an oxygen mask over her face, and wheeled her out.

Chapter 20

PERSPECTIVE

A ngie approached Enrico with trepidation, his face flushed from his recent show of bravery. The way he thought on his feet in a time of crisis was admirable, and she saw him in a different light. Enrico was a policeman who saved a woman's life without thinking about anything else. While he focused on the woman, Angie caught a glimpse of fear in his eyes. He was afraid for the stranger. Enrico really did care about helping others. It looked as though the woman would be fine, thanks to Enrico.

He was talking to his friends, Ray, and Lorenzo, so she maintained her distance until he excused himself and approached her. "Hey, Angie. I wasn't sure if you were coming."

"You did great out there. Saved that woman's life. Are you okay? You look a bit rattled."

He nodded. "I'm fine. I thought she was a goner there for a while, but I refused to let her die on my watch. I just don't know how she suddenly had a heart attack, but it happens. I'll go visit her later and check-in."

"Well, you should be commended. No doubt you'll be in the papers tomorrow. I don't usually read the papers, but I will tomorrow."

"Thanks, Angie." He pondered. "Now, how about a coffee? I could sure use one before I leave."

"Okay."

As they moved towards the cafe, the commotion of the event resumed. Policemen huddled around the viewing public, some of them having their photographs taken, holding Styrofoam cups in their hands and chattering with co-workers.

Enrico walked alongside her until they reached the nearby cafe, hi-fiving a man who must've been the owner. He faced her. "Take a seat over there and I'll bring them over."

Sitting in the cafe, she lifted her shoulders and watched Enrico laughing with the owner who sported a moustache with greying hair. They seemed to be close as he later bent down low to say hello to a young girl of about five. She must've been the man's granddaughter. He reached into his back pocket and handed her a lollypop. The girl's eyes lit up like diamonds. Did he buy the candy just for the girl or did he happen to have a lollypop in his pocket?

The young girl unwrapped her candy and sucked it with vigour, then rushed into the back of the cafe. Enrico retrieved the tray of hot drinks and made his way over to Angie with a smile that made her melt inside.

He set the drinks on the table. "Here's your cappuccino." He sat down opposite Angie. "I have about twenty minutes before I need to get back, but we can at least enjoy a coffee."

"Thanks, Enrico." She rested her back against the padded chair. "So how do you do this job, day in day out? Don't you get traumatised a lot?"

He chuckled. "My love for helping others overrides all that. We have a great psychologist on the force, and I have supportive friends and family. I am trained to deal with crisis, so I have adapted, but there are days when you wish you could just take a break from life. Days when you're sick of seeing death and destruction, but they're very few and far between. How about you? What did you do before the bookstore?"

She wasn't sure about wanting the focus on herself but pushed down her ambivalence. "I was a marketing executive and loved the chase of presenting to clients for their business, and being challenged to up my game each time I designed a board to present my ideas. I liked the excitement and the adrenaline rush I got from the chase, but after a while I found I was losing my soul. It didn't mean much to me anymore. Who was I helping, really? The rich and the wealthy to get even wealthier by making higher profits each year. I wanted to be more grounded and share my love of books with people, and give exceptional customer service. That's important to me—making others excited by a book and giving them that escape."

"Well, you've accomplished a lot. I can imagine how great you'd be at your job in marketing. I could tell even at school how smart you were. You're even smarter now."

Angie was having a great time until he mentioned school. How would he know she was smart when he never got to know her then? Had Jake revealed everything about her to Enrico?

She quickly drank down her coffee, burning her lips in the process. The awkward silence between them was unnerving until she finished her drink and got up. "I have to go. Thanks for the drink."

Enrico frowned, tilting his head. "Wait. I'll walk with you."

She shook her head. "No need. Thanks." Angie scurried out of the cafe, bypassed the remaining few police officers talking to a few people, then headed into the fresh air for much-needed breathing space. Angie swallowed, not sure why she came. Her business cards remained in her bag, forgotten the moment she saw Enrico. She should have never come.

Chapter 21

DECISION

Enrico squared his shoulders as he sat at the table with Angie and Jenna. Tim spoke quietly to a DJ on the phone while Susie made notes. Gina and Ray sat in front of the computer, updating news of the venue on the basic website they created. His mind wandered over to Angie whose demeanour had changed so abruptly while having coffee at Barkly Square. It must've been when he brought up how smart she was in school, probably wondering how he knew that. They had had a few classes together at school and he had noticed how she occasionally answered challenging questions by the teacher. At least she was softening towards him, and hopefully, seeing his true colours now.

Gina called out to Enrico. "So you're sure you want this Docklands catering company, or do you have other places in mind to still visit?"

He shook his head. "No, it sounds like the others are happy with the type of food this place specialises in. We just need to choose from the variety of menus they have." He watched Angie flicking through a menu to select the array of buffet foods, some of which they had tasted. Jenna looked at the menu over her shoulder, then looked up at Enrico and grinned. He wondered if she was surprised by Angie's slight change of attitude towards him, which may have had something to do with that poor woman having a heart attack. Enrico had checked on her and Judy was recovering.

Pointing her finger at one of the dishes on the menu, Angie straightened up in her chair. Smells of lavender and musk wafted in the air and his body relaxed beside her. He wondered if they could start to be at least friendly towards each other, if not actual friends.

"What about having the hors d'oeuvres to start with, then a variety of these chicken, lamb, and beef dishes for the main so that we're catering to different tastes?"

Enrico nodded. "Hmm. Sounds good. What do you think, Jenna?"

She sipped her water and threw a piece of bread into her mouth, chewing as she spoke. "I think it sounds like a plan, but perhaps instead of the lamb we can go for one of those seafood dishes, as at least half of those coming don't like lamb. It is easier to go with seafood. Although having about one hundred and eighty people coming to this reunion, you're bound to not please everyone. But we can give it a good hot try."

Angie beamed. "Okay." She pointed to a seafood dish on the menu. "What about this one?"

Enrico touched her shoulder but she flinched. "Great idea, Angie. I like that one." He sat back and realised what an idiot he was. It was a reflex action, as he didn't want to touch her without her consent. He violated her personal boundary. "Sorry," he whispered.

"I have to get on with this," Angie said flatly.

Jenna agreed. "Now, we just need a few different desserts."

Enrico watched Angie as she wrote down the entire menu to send back to the venue who would need to prepare the food at least a few days before the reunion. Then half an hour went by and everyone was ready to leave.

Jenna stood up. "Thanks for your help, guys. We got a lot done today, so we won't need to meet for at least another month. Email me any more ideas you have, and Gina and Ray, start working on those invitations to send out." As they waved goodbye to Angie then ambled out the door, Enrico stayed behind.

"I'll help you clean up."

"Thanks. I've got cling wrap in that cupboard over there," said Angie.

He covered the bread and variety of cheeses and placed them in the fridge while Angie collected the jugs of water and disposable cups, throwing the latter into a nearby bin.

She stood awkwardly in front of the kettle, staring at it for a few seconds. Lifting her shoulders, she turned to him. "Would you like a coffee?"

Enrico's heart warmed. "I would love one. Thanks." He sat back at the table and waited until she set his mug in front of him. She sat across from him with her own mug. "We did get a lot done today, didn't we?"

Angie pressed her lips together, taking a sip of her coffee with its steam permeating the air. "We did."

"You seem to know food. Have you worked in the industry, or do you just like cooking or watching shows about food?"

Angie's eyes peered into the distance. "I love trying out different recipes and remember how my mum used to make the best shortbread. She taught me how to cook and that was how we bonded after she stopped...drinking."

"How is your mum?"

"She is great. Healthier than ever, and her and my stepfather, Jack, are amazing parents. We had a rough road, but now she is sober and I couldn't be more grateful."

"I'm so happy for you, Angie. You deserve it." The next reunion meeting was a month away. To him, it felt like forever until he would see Angie again. Worse, they didn't really have a reason to keep seeing each other with the caterer and venue chosen. Before he could stop himself, he said, "Listen, I was curious about whether...whether you'd like to have lunch one day." Her face looked blank. He tried to recover. "I need to get working on the DJ table, and we can help set up the building next door. I've got the supplies. I might need to make a buffet or coffee bar, but these won't take me long. We can have lunch on a Saturday if you like and I can get to work. What do you think?"

"Thanks, Enrico. I would appreciate you making those tables. Perhaps do a coffee bar instead of a buffet." She rose. "Anyway, I'm beat. I think I will call it a night."

He hid his disappointment. "Of course. I'll let you know about lunch."

Angie showed a hint of a smile as she walked him to the door. "Bye, Enrico."

"Bye, Angie." Their eyes locked until she broke his gaze and closed the door. He walked to his car with his head held high, wondering if she was slowly warming up to him. Only time would tell.

Chapter 22

PLEASANT LUNCH

Angie took a fifty-dollar note from a customer, gave out the change, and put a hardcover fiction book into an environmentally friendly bag. "Thanks for coming. Enjoy the book."

The customer smiled and retrieved the bag. "Oh, I'll be back. You have such a range of books here. Thank you."

Angie smiled, her heart lifting at the compliment. She turned to Maddy who gave her a wink as she priced books at their discounted price. Normally Angie struggled with Mondays, but with Enrico on her mind she had a bit more of a spring in her step. She hadn't seen him since Wednesday night at the meeting, and she wondered if he'd make good on his promise about taking her out for lunch. In spite of the awkwardness between them in the staff room, he was working hard to make amends for his past indiscretion. She could give him a chance and see whether he was as skilled as he said he was in woodwork. What she wasn't comfortable with, was how each time she saw him her stomach fluttered, or her hands became sweaty whenever he gazed strongly into her eyes. It must be the pain of the past; that was all. She still wasn't over it, but it was a start.

Maddy put aside the price gun and dusted the bookshelf behind the counter. "Great compliment. And we are doing a lot better with sales. We could later expand with a coffee and couch area, particularly if we want to rent out our space for events. We could charge a higher fee with those additions. What do you think?"

"Sounds great, but we need to get the book side of things well-established first. And see if the events space works. One thing at a time, but we can look into it later." Angie served another customer and placed the one hundred dollar bill into the cash register. Another sale with the customer buying several books. She took a breath and scanned passersby strolling across the walk out front of the shop, hoping for another influx of customers. The marketing of the reunion helped to bring in a few extra customers; a few of the friendlier students from high school visited recently.

A man in a police uniform came into the store. Her heart raced as Enrico waltzed in, wearing his blue police uniform fitted snugly around his chest. He looked handsome, rugged, and hot. Her body temperature rose ten-fold. *Get a grip, girl!*

He grinned and stood opposite her across the counter. "Hi girls, I hope you don't mind me dropping in." He eyed Angie. "Would you like to have lunch? I have an hour to spare before I have to get back to work."

Angie was speechless, still in awe at the way he wore his police uniform. She focused on Maddy who nodded. "Okay. But I thought you were working next door on the tables." "I was meant to have the day off but I got called in, so I'll come back before you close. I managed to get someone to cover me for the last few hours of my shift. Will that be okay?"

Angie leaned beneath the counter, opened up the cabinet, and reached for her bag. "That's fine." Turning to her friend, she said, "Thanks, Maddy. I'll be back soon."

She grinned cheekily. "Take your time, girl. I'll hold the fort here. No worries."

She stood at Enrico's side and together they walked outside the shop. She felt people watching them. No doubt, anyone walking with a policeman would easily stand out.

They headed to the nearby cafe where Enrico ordered a chicken schnitzel burger and Angie ordered a beef burger for herself. The lunch crowd left only one table free. The table was in the back and a little quieter than the front part of the cafe.

Enrico's gaze fixed on her as he sat opposite. She ignored her tight stomach. "I am glad we can get to know each other, Angie." She winced, not sure she trusted getting to know him that well. "I mean, given that the reunion's not too far away, we can focus on planning the set-up of your building next door."

She nodded. "I appreciate you helping out with the tables. But only if you've got the time." Angie rubbed her hands together until the waiter brought their food and iced tea. The waiter left with a nod.

Enrico picked up his drink. "It's what I love to do. When I'm banging away with nails and creating something, I get into this zone where nothing bothers me. I am totally calm and in sync with everything."

Angie tilted her head. "Why are you really doing this, Enrico?"

He hesitated, looking past her. "Friends help each other out."

She cleared her throat. "Are we friends?"

"I would like us to be. Make a fresh start. What do you think?"

Angie's heart warmed, her body responding in ways she didn't want it to. She needed to change the subject. "Since we're making a fresh start, and I shared about my family, tell me more about your family."

Enrico's eyes lit up. "My mother is retired and has strong beliefs within her Italian group of friends. She clashes with my sister Stella at times." His eyes moved down. "My father died while serving his time as a police officer. A robbery gone wrong." He cleared his throat, his voice becoming heavy with emotion. "I love my work because he inspired me in the field. And I looked up to him."

Angie gasped, understanding all too well the loss of a father. "I'm sorry. It's hard when you lose a parent. I'm sure he'd be very proud of you and what you've accomplished."

He sighed. "Thanks, Angie." They dug into their burgers in silence until mayonnaise dripped down Angie's chin. He picked up a napkin. "You have mayonnaise on your lip." He held up the napkin. "Do you mind?" She shook her head. He dabbed it across her lip. The whole world ceased to exist for Angie in that moment. She gazed at the way his lips parted. His eyes fixed on hers and she got lost in them. The room spun around her with a dizzying sensation when the reverie broke.

"Excuse me," said the waiter. "Is there anything else you'd like?"

Angie swallowed. "No thanks." She blushed and averted her eyes.

Once they finished their lunch, he walked her back to the shop and shook her hand. "I'll come back to the shop at around five and start working on the table next door.""Okay." As she walked back into the store, she was in a daze, her mixed emotions unsettling her.

Chapter 23

TEAMWORK

Angie squared her shoulders later that day as she waved goodbye to Maddy after the closing of the bookstore. While waiting for Enrico to return, she got a notification on her phone. "Sorry, running an hour late. Got caught up in a case. Can come back another time if you have plans. Let me know."

She shook her head with a sigh. Typical! Even though she didn't have plans tonight, he was still controlling her. Now, she needed to decide whether she wanted to hang around or go home. But what would she be going home to? A movie and a small frozen dinner without company. Jimmy was going out tonight so she would be home alone. Normally, she enjoyed a quiet night at home, but lately, she started to wonder what it would be like to have Enrico sitting on her couch and talking like old friends. Crazy! They might have made some headway during lunch earlier today, but Enrico had a lot to make up for.

Angie made her way to the staffroom, cleaned out the small fridge and washed a few dishes in the sink. She picked up her phone and sent Enrico a quick text. *I'll be here.* Then she made her way to the building next door, retrieving her key out of her pocket and unlocked it. Her eyes roamed the dust-filled skirting boards, the bare white-washed walls with two lone hooks, the dusty matted floorboards, and assorted cables lining the ground. She picked up two landscape paintings she bought for the bare walls and hung them up on the hooks. With a sigh, she turned at a knock on the door. Her heart beat fast and her hands sweated as she swung open the door. He was no longer in his police uniform but wore casual jeans which hugged his body like a second skin and a white fitted t-shirt that showed his abs. He carried a toolbox. She wondered if the heating was on.

"Sorry I'm late, Angie. I had to process someone at the station but he wasn't behaving. And thanks for waiting."

"Come in."

He dropped his toolbox on the floor. "I have to get the timber from my car. It's already been cut to size. I'll be back."

"Do you need help?"

"Sure. Lorenzo was going to help, but something came up. You don't mind being my apprentice tonight, do you?"

She shrugged, thinking she had nothing better to do. "It's fine." She followed him to his car and picked up two pieces of mahogany wood out of his boot while Enrico carried several more. They wandered back and forth a few times, carrying a drill, hammer, varnish, and paint until he was ready to start. She watched him pick up a drill.

"Would you mind holding the wood while I drill?" She nodded and made her way over, standing close to him as he drilled nails into the timber. He briefly looked up. "So no plans tonight?"

She shook her head. "No plans." Averting the focus from herself, she shifted. "Who taught you how to woodwork?" A piece of wood against the wall fell and she turned back and rested it against a chair behind her.

"My dad did when I was ten and I've loved it ever since."

"It is a great skill to have. If only my father taught me something. But my stepfather, Jack's a different story. He's the father I should have had from the beginning." Why did she even share that?

Enrico picked up a piece of wood and joined it with the other piece. "I am sorry to hear that. But better late than never." As he drilled the wood to join the other two pieces, she couldn't help but notice the way his biceps expanded underneath his t-shirt, and the way his full lips pressed tightly together.

She kept her grip on the timber. "I am lucky now that we're a united front." She realised that she could use a coffee bar for an author signing that was coming up and wondered if he could make it by then. "Listen, Enrico. I have this author event in a few weeks. Would you by any chance be able to make that coffee bar by then? I could use something for tea and coffee facilities for the guests. But only if you can make it by that time."

He put down the two pieces and picked up a drill bit. Looking up, he said, "Does that mean you're using this building or the bookshop space for the event?"

"It'll be in this space for the book readings, and customers can buy the books in the bookshop."

Enrico peered into the distance for a moment. "I should be able to get it done by then. I would love to, Angie. As I said, it is my passion and it won't take me long at all. That is something I can make from home and bring it by. Besides, you could use that for the reunion too."

She nodded. "I guess so. Thanks, Enrico. We are lucky to have someone with carpentry skills. I struggle to even hammer a nail into a plank of wood."

He laughed. "I would be happy to teach you." As he joined more wood to create a shelf underneath the table, she leaned back and jabbed herself with a plank. A sharp pain penetrated her back. Quickly, he put down his drill and lifted up her hand. "Are you okay?"

Angie winced at the throbbing pain in her back. If only she hadn't rested that piece of wood directly behind her. "The pain will pass. It's fine."

He moved closer. "Where are you hurt? Can I check where the pain is?" She nodded. He knit his brows as she sat down on the floor and rested her back against the wall. His hands were tender as he pushed gently into the lower part of her back, his eyes focused on her. She ignored the tingles in her body and the flutter in her stomach. "Is it sore there?"

"A little, but it's more of an acute pain, so it will pass."

He proceeded to massage the area. "Just rest here a moment and give it time. If the pain gets worse, let me know. I shouldn't be too long to at least get the basics of this table done tonight. I can varnish it and do the rest later."

A part of her felt guilty for hurting herself like that. Something that was avoidable if she'd kept her surroundings safe. Now she could no longer help him until the pain subsided. But then again, she didn't owe him anything.

As she watched him get back to work, she realised that she hadn't once thought about Enrico as the bully from her past. She saw him as Enrico the carpenter and policeman with a tender side.

Chapter 24

RELAXED MOMENT

Angie's fingers shook as she stepped into a cafe at The Docklands, close to the restaurant and catering company they were using for the reunion. Enrico called to invite her over for a coffee and to pick up a few of her business cards to distribute to people he knew in the community. In spite of her doubts, she hated to admit to herself that she sensed a coldness at his absence in the last week. The way he tended to her back pain at the bookshop, and the way he took the time to make a DJ table for the reunion made her see him in a different light. Her mind lingered over what he thought about the latest TV shows or his opinion about the current state of the economy. She was even curious about his morning routine and how he interacted with his mother and sister. Did he think about his late father often?

Shaking her thoughts away, Angie focused on the here and now. The cafe buzzed with noise. She made her way towards Enrico, whose eyes followed her, surveying her from top to bottom and arousing her attraction towards him. She still had doubts about whether they could be close friends, but after what happened at the coffee with a cop event, she owed it to him to at least see whether he was a different person.

He wore a white shirt pressed against his sturdy chest, and tight-fitted ripped blue jeans. She wondered what it would be like to run her hands over his muscles and what it would be like to kiss him around his biceps. With a resigned sigh, she returned to the present. It had been too long since she'd been on a date.

Sitting opposite him, Enrico watched her get comfortable. "Thanks for meeting me, Angie." The young waiter took their orders of cafe latte and cappuccino then left with a grin. "Okay, so tell me what you do for fun, or how you chill out?"

She lifted an eyebrow. "I like keeping busy. I'd be bored staying home, but when I am, I enjoy reading and movies, and I like going to the gym, too."

He eyed her closely. "I love the gym too, and in my line of work, it's a requirement to stay fit. What about movies? What kind do you like?"

"Psychological thrillers and romance," said Angie. "Anything that keeps me up at night and has intrigue and suspense." The waiter set down their hot drinks.

Enrico added sugar to his latte, stirring it without taking his eyes off Angie. "Yes, the very dark thrillers, and so long as the romance has an interesting plotline, who doesn't love a captivating romance?"

They spent the next hour laughing about movies and getting on to controversial issues about the state of the economy, and how domestic violence was all too prevalent in today's society. He must have seen a lot of abuse and violence in his line of work. Enrico stood up. "How about a walk in the park?"

She nodded. "I'd like that if you're free for the rest of the night."

"I'm good."

They made their way towards the park and reached the tree-lined path which led them to a flock of pigeons and square blocks of concrete. Angie walked alongside Enrico and accidentally bumped into him, a strong tingle permeating her abdomen. A group of people huddled and threw a ball, while families with children ran after those who headed closer to the road.

The winter sun on her skin was warm, and the blinding light made her squint as Enrico touched the small of her back, leading her to a bench.

"Would you like to sit?" Enrico asked.

"Sure." They sat side by side in comfortable silence. "Tell me why you work as a policeman. What made you decide to work in the field?"

"I love my job even though it has its risks. I'm working my way up to detective, but I worry about missing those first responder calls and patrolling the streets. I love the adrenaline rush from bringing those criminals down, especially those who hurt kids. It gets to me the most, and I struggle to keep a level head at times. The reward I get when I've saved someone from a fate worse than death or death itself is the biggest joy. I guess you can say that my father inspired me to help people. He never gave Stella and me a free ride, and we worked hard at school and work. He taught us the value of effort and diligence. But when he died, all his training went out the window. It was like I lost a part of me, and I became a jerk."

Angie pursed her lips. "He sounds like a great man." She cleared her throat. "I know you mentioned having a psychologist at work, but how else do you deal with the trauma?"

He peered towards the people kicking a ball around. "I go to the gym, read books, and talk to friends or my mum, and as I said before, I love woodwork too. It's the feeling I get when I touch a close-grained piece of wood, like basswood used in carving. And then there's chip-carving, which is a style of decorative carving where I take out the chips instead of shaving the wood." He frowned. "I'm sorry. I get carried away when talking about wood. You must be bored out of your mind."

She shook her head, her mind wandering towards his lips, imagining what they would taste like on hers. "Not at all, and they're good strategies." Her hand rested on her thigh, and he placed his own hand on top. She savoured the gentleness of his touch and a lightness filled her chest. It was as though their hands melted into each other.

The sound of a child's laughter in the distance made her come to her senses. Abruptly, she flicked her hand away and rose.

He got up from the bench too and gave her a smile which didn't reach his eyes. "I am sorry if I was out of line. I just remembered that I was meant to grab a few of your business cards. Do you have any? I can pass them around to a few of my contacts in the community. We got distracted the last time at the coffee with a cop event."

She pulled out a stack of business cards from her bag and handed them to him. "I appreciate it," said Angie.

His eyes were a shade darker. "I had a great time with you, as usual, and I would like for us to be friends. Don't you want that too?"

"Enrico, I can't do this right now. I'm not sure about anything, least of all how I feel about friendship." In silence, they made their way to their respective cars. Angie pointed to hers. "My car's over there, but thanks for the nice afternoon."

He gave her an awkward smile. "Can I see you again, Angie?"

Angie swallowed. "Maybe." She walked to her car without looking back. One step at a time.

Chapter 25

A STEP CLOSER

Enrico stood in front of a local cafe the next day, cuffing a stout man sporting tattoos and earrings. He stood glaring and scoffing as if he had been wronged.

"I ain't done nothing," said the man. "Just minding my business when this bloke comes into the cafe and asks to speak to me. I come to the front and he reckons I slept with his wife. When I denied it, he made a swing at me and I defended myself."

Enrico shook his head, turning to Peter, who knit his brows. "We have witnesses who said you threw the first punch, Wally." He avoided passersby gawking at the intimidating and solid man. "You can get processed at the station and answer further questions there. Now, let's move."

An ambulance arrived, and two paramedics laid a scrawny man onto a stretcher, his eyes bloody, his face bruised, and part of his ear lobe bitten off. Enrico pushed Wally into the police car and drove off with Peter in the passenger seat. The short trip to the police station was uneventful as Wally continued to proclaim his innocence. The man who accused him of sleeping with his wife gave Wally a swollen lip in self-defence. Enrico didn't doubt Wally lied and slept with a married woman.

The whole situation reminded him of his friend, Jake, who had betrayed him by sleeping with Gina, his girlfriend at the time. It wasn't that he cared about Gina so much, but more about how his best friend could go behind his back and pretend nothing happened. Enrico had swung a few punches of his own at a man he had deemed to be a loyal friend. Boy, had he been wrong. He should have seen that when Jake did what he did to Angie. Loyalty was high on his list of values, and he understood how Angie could see that he didn't have good values in high school. He hadn't been a good person then, so he hadn't earned the right to be treated well by Angie. No doubt, those words and images still lingered in her mind. He struggled to deny his feelings towards her; he knew she wasn't ready for anything more, and he had to respect that.

Enrico parked inside the precinct, exited the car, and processed Wally with Peter alongside him. His phone buzzed in his pocket. Looking at the display, he frowned. *Angie!* Turning to Peter, Enrico pushed Wally further inside the station. "Would you mind finishing processing him? I've got to take this. It shouldn't take long."

He nodded. "No worries, boss."

Enrico took a deep breath. He had left Angie a phone message and she was returning his call. "Angie, hi. We need to talk. Can we meet on Sunday? At the St Kilda Pier?"

She hesitated. "I guess that should be fine, Enrico."

Her voice made pleasant tingles skate across his skin. He wanted to explain how he felt. "What time can you meet?"

"How about one o'clock?

"Sure. I'll see you then." His body was on fire at the idea of seeing her again.

They said their goodbyes and Enrico ended the call, a rush of heat penetrating his chest.

Chapter 26

NEW BEGINNING

Angie's body was taut as she stepped onto the St Kilda pier, her feet feeling like lead over rough and uneven ground. Her fingers slid across the rail as she gazed over the calm waters, heading towards the Pavilion with Enrico. Grey clouds filled the blue sky with imminent rain. Her eyes roamed the natural surroundings as she took small breaths to calm her nerves.

They walked behind the kiosk and leaned against the fence before entering the shop to order comfort food. Angie ordered a cafe latte and Enrico ordered an espresso coffee with cheesecake for both of them. Moving towards a table, Angie stared out over the beachside through the large windows letting in soft sunlight with a subtle warmth over her body.

Angie sat back on the hard-backed chair and watched passersby, listening to the buzz of activity and comforting noise, and inhaling the aroma of coffee beans, cinnamon, and spices. She focused on Enrico, who smiled at the waiter bringing their hot beverages and cheesecake set on two small plates. Angie pushed her fork into the soft cheese and crumb texture and took a bite. It was delicious and would go straight to her hips. She played with the strands of her long hair after eating more of her dessert, her eyes closing as she tasted it. "Heaven!"

Enrico shook his head, looking at his dessert rather than eating it. "It does look good."

Angie held her stomach. "I'm so full just looking at the rest of this." She fought back the tightness in her chest and knotted vocal cords, realising they were lightening the mood before delving into deeper issues.

Enrico pressed his spoon into his dessert while Angie focused on the way his lips wrapped around the cheesecake, his tongue flicking in and out. He looked up at her with a cheeky grin as if he noticed she'd been staring. "Do you hate me, Angie?"

Angie clutched her mug and sipped, the steam heating her skin. "A part of me cannot shake this off." She picked at her fingernails and played origami with her napkin. She didn't know how to express herself when so many emotions ran rampant inside her.

Enrico gazed into her eyes. "You didn't answer my question. I'd like to know if we're on the same page. Do you hate me?"

"No, I don't," said Angie. "Not anymore." She straightened her posture. "Seeing how you love helping people and being on this re-union committee shows you have changed. But the past still hurts."

He focused on patrons drifting into the cafe, some with children and others coupled up. "That is a good start." He looked into his hands then faced her. "I...I care about you, Angie."

She held her breath for a moment. Her hair lifted on her nape and arms, and her throat felt parched. What did he expect her to say when she still had mixed emotions about him? How could she trust him fully or feel much when she couldn't see past the hurt? "I see."

Enrico's eyes turned a shade darker. "I'm sorry if I made you uncomfortable." Angie stayed quiet. "I don't know what else to tell you, Angie. But I am not that guy anymore."

Angie nodded. "I know. I can see that now."

He knit his brows and chewed on a piece of cheesecake. Wiping his mouth, his eyes roamed her face. "I didn't mean to put any pressure on you, Angie." He cleared his throat. "I have started on the coffee bar for your event and the reunion. The DJ table is almost done, so what else do you need for the room?"

She sighed. "Nothing else at this stage. We just need to prepare the room. I know Tim was looking at audiovisual equipment as he's pretty tech-savvy."

Enrico nodded. "Are you sure? You haven't seen the depth of my creative design skills. I'm happy to do more for the space."

"All good. Thanks." She knew what he was doing, easing his guilt, but a part of her was grateful for his woodwork designs.

He beamed. "Are you planning on doing anything with that building after the reunion? Is that meant for you to expand the bookshop?"

Angie hesitated, wondering how much to tell him. But he was helping her with marketing her business and getting the word around, and this was part of that. "I plan to use the space for events in the future. Have a venue for companies who need a promotional event or want to use it for training. Jack was kind enough to buy it for me, and I plan on making it work for an extension of my current bookshop. I mean, I already use the bookshop for author signings, so why not have the extra space for events?"

His eyes glowed. "It sounds like a great idea. All the more reason a coffee bar would entice companies to use the space. If you have a musical event, they have the DJ table to use."

"I guess you're right. I just hope it all comes together."

After they finished their drinks and dessert, Enrico got up and paid the bill. He led her back outside alongside the pier holding the small of her back. It felt right, his skin arousing her and triggering her desire for something more.

Angie swallowed, barely blinking as their eyes locked, but she moved on ahead until reaching the shore of the beach. She sat on the sand in a spot with a little privacy from the roaming public. Enrico joined her, their thighs brushing.

Angie broke the ice. "When did things change for you? Your outlook about what you'd done back then?"

His eyes turned a shade darker. "It took about a couple of years after I joined the police force. Seeing how people were abused by bullies led me to realise that I had been that person. I felt the suffering of others, and I knew deep down that my anger at the death of my father had contributed to my bullying. I wish I understood what you might've been going through then." He knit his brows. "I was young and stupid and never once realised how hard it was for you with your mum. I am so sorry. If I could take it all back, I would."

Angie's heart warmed at his heartfelt confession. He was young then. Could she blame him for being naive and stupid as a teenager who only wanted to have fun, and not have to worry about a girl who appeared distant and had an alcoholic mother? She had had baggage that a normal male teenager would struggle with. Why would a teenager want the burden of problems? She smiled. "Thanks for your honesty, Enrico."

His eyes lit up. "I appreciate you saying that."

A magnetic pull drew her towards him as he intertwined his left fingers with hers, his right thumb and index finger pulling her chin towards him. Parting his lips, he inched his way towards her and kissed her, gently at first, then with hunger and desire. Angie had never been kissed like this before, and she was floating on a cloud as his strong hands pulled her closer and explored more deeply into her mouth.

Angie's head took over as she realised she wasn't ready for this. She pulled away from him and averted her eyes. "I don't think you should have done that."Enrico swallowed. "I'm sorry if I was out of line. I guess I misinterpreted what I thought was a moment." He stared out over the ocean as if in deep thought.

Angie had no words, and watched the rolling waves, the soaring seagulls, the passersby strolling along the sand, and the light breeze that promised a warm night. She clutched her chest and calmed her rapid breathing. It was time to go home.

Chapter 27

MOTHERLY ADVICE

A week later, Angie rang the doorbell at her mother's house and put her hands in the pockets of her jeans. Her mind couldn't stop seeing the image of her kiss with Enrico, the gentle way he held her, and the way he made her feel. It was sublime, but she didn't want it to be. What if he ended up hurting her again?

Her mother answered after a minute. "Darling. So good to see you. Come in." She followed her to the kitchen, where the clean white floors were shiny and dust-free as she glided across to a chair. Her mother's brown leather bag rested on a glossy white bench sitting below double cupboards, and an artificial plant sat on the side of the tall fridge.

Her mother put on the kettle and smiled. "I'll make us a coffee. How have you been? You look pensive."

She gave her mother a stern look, envious of her mother's refreshed and relaxed appearance. "I'm fine, Mum. How's Jack?"

She took out two mugs from an overhead cupboard. "Okay. Work has been a little quiet, but it should pick up after a bit of advertising. He's gone into Shepparton today to talk to a new client, trying to drum up more business that way too. So what brings you by? You don't normally drop by this early on a Sunday."

Before Angie could respond, her mother placed a mug of coffee on the table then sat opposite. Her mother set down her own coffee and then took a sip. "Here you go. Now spill."

Angie wrapped her hands around the mug, savouring the warmth and comfort of a strong cup of coffee. "Tell me again why you drank, Mum. I am trying to understand how people change. I mean, Jack took a chance on you when you were an alcoholic."

Her mother clasped her hands in her lap. Her gaze darted and she adjusted her clothes and fidgeted. "Wow! That's a lot in one sentence, dear. Now, where do I start?" She took a breath. "Your father was difficult, Angie. He was emotionally abusive and put me down every opportunity he got. He was always angry and put us in debt because of his damn gambling addiction. The pressure of having a family, working odd shift hours, I struggled to cope, and I drank, recovered, and drank again. Each time I had a stressor I drank. Jack was my lifeline and he loved me which was why he took a chance on me."

She took a breath, fighting a quaking bottom lip. "I'd like to apologise for embarrassing you at school in front of your friends. I'm sorry for being too drunk to attend your graduation or other school events. I will always regret losing those moments." Her eyes shone momentarily. "And as for you wanting to understand how people change, they do to some extent. I mean, someone's personality can be static, but it's about being the best version of yourself, given the personality you were born with. Are we talking about Enrico here?"

Angie nodded.

"I am glad you've started a friendship with Enrico. I always knew he wasn't really a bully, but had succumbed to peer pressure. And he lost his father too at the time. Nothing a young boy should have to endure. He has a heart. I can tell. A few times I picked you up, drunk, and his friends smirked in my direction, but he had this sad expression and shoved them, shaking his head and leaving them to their glaring at me. He didn't belong in that group, but teenagers have a lot to learn. What he did was inexcusable then, but I could tell he was different. And I really am sorry I drank and contributed to the bullying."

Angie's chest hitched. "No, Mum. It wasn't your fault. Alcoholism is a disease and you fought it. Put the blame where it belongs—on those bullies."

Her mother reached out for her hand. "I love you, Angie. So much. Never doubt that I always loved you even when I wasn't in my right mind."

"It's fine, Mum. You were sober for a lot of years too, and you did your best."

"Oh, Angie." She pulled her daughter into a tight hug. "You are the best daughter anyone could've asked for, and I definitely don't deserve you." Breaking away, Angie stood up and paced. "Angie. How are things with Enrico? What's going on?"

Angie's eyes turned inward, contemplating. "We kissed, but I'm not sure it was the right thing to do." He promised to give her space. She always knew he wasn't inherently bad, even in high school, but hearing about his behaviour from her mother made it all the more real. Did he really have genuine feelings for her? Was it her past that coloured her present situation with Enrico?

Her mother tilted her head. "If you kissed him, then you must think he's changed. How do you feel about him?"

Angie swallowed. "I care about him. A lot, and that's what scares me, Mum."

"Let me tell you something, Angie. That boy has a heart and helps out the community, and now you can only go with your intuition. Do what feels right, and don't let Enrico or anyone pressure you into anything you're not ready to do."

Angie nodded. "Thanks, Mum."

She wondered whether Enrico would call her, or should she call him?

Later that day, Angie lay on her bed, again thinking about Enrico and the kiss they had shared. She stared at her phone resting on the bedside table, wondering if she should call him. Before she could decide to call, it buzzed. She lifted up her body and draped her legs over to the side of the bed. The display showed Enrico. Answering the call, she held her breath. "Hi, Enrico."

"Angie, hi. I hope it's okay that I called you?"

Angie swallowed. "Sure." Her voice caught in her throat and she didn't know what to say.

"Look, the reason I'm calling is I wanted to apologise for kissing you. I didn't mean to rush you, and I realised later you weren't ready. I thought we had a moment and I acted without thinking."

She didn't expect an admission by Enrico. "It's fine, Enrico. I would like us to be friends, but anything more than that, I don't know at this stage. I hope you understand."

"Of course. I'd like us to be friends too."

She wanted to extend an olive branch, given the way he had apologised and helped her by creating the DJ table and coffee bar. The least she could do was invite him to the book signing she mentioned to him a couple of weeks ago. "Listen, before you hang up. I wanted to remind you about the book signing for this author next Saturday. Are you still free?"

"I'll be there, Angie. Text me the details and I'll come by early to help out." He paused. "Have a good night."

"You too, Enrico."

Chapter 28

AUTHOR
SIGNING

The following Saturday, Enrico pinned a huge author banner across the entrance to Angie's bookstore and climbed down the ladder. He eyed the massive sign. "Book Signing, J.D Larss, Second Chance.' Her name was Janie, but J.D was her brand for her romance stories. He wasn't surprised that she'd invited him to this event, given that he helped create designs for the reunion, but in this way, they were testing out her space for future new business.

He couldn't get the kiss out of his mind. He loved the way Angie bit into her bottom lip when she was nervous. He loved the way her breath hitched when she was hesitant, and he loved how her lips tasted on his own. He dreamt about her at night and thought about her in the mornings. It was crazy.

Pushing away thoughts, Enrico entered the building next door and arranged plastic chairs around the small table filled with stacks of novels, business cards, labelled pens, and notebooks. Janie stood opposite Angie who peered over towards him briefly. Enrico walked towards them and wheeled his new coffee bar in the corner of the room which was made of a Baltic birch plywood and featured a table with two shelves beneath each other. He turned to them, having met J.D Larss earlier. "I can go and get the coffee facilities if you like."

Angie nodded. "Thanks, Enrico. I appreciate that."

Janie had long, wavy hair, blue eyes, and a robust build. "I appreciate your help, Enrico. As an author, I don't know how well I'm going to do in terms of sales. I still need to build my brand, you know?"

Enrico grinned. "I am sure you'll do fine." He spotted a few people through the window heading to the bookshop. "I can see a few people coming now, so it's a good start." The author made her way to the table and added several more books from a box beside it. Angie and Enrico headed over to the staff room and hefted a tray of cups, two small kettles, and tea and coffee facilities. "When is the book signing meant to start, Angie?"

She placed the coffee jar next to the tea box in the room. "In about twenty minutes, but some have obviously come by early." Her fingers played with the positioning of the jar of sugar as if she couldn't get it right.

"Oh, my goodness, Angie. You have OCD, don't you? The sugar was fine where it was. Don't worry so much."

"Hmm. So you think." She shook her head. "I don't doubt you have obsessive traits over your woodwork or police work."

"It comes with the territory, I guess. But a jar of sugar? Really?"

Angie chuckled, her eyes glistening as the morning sun reflected against the window. He liked seeing her like this: in control and organising an event which helped others' businesses. His hand yearned to reach out and pull that small hair strand out of her eyes or to touch her full lips as she leaned closer towards him. Clearing her throat, she turned away. "I better get to Maddy and get this event started."

Enrico nodded. "I'll be right behind you." As she walked ahead of him, he wondered how long it would take for her to feel totally comfortable in his presence. He didn't know what more he could do to prove he was trustworthy.

As they headed to the door, Angie opened it and ushered in the group of women and several men inside who took their seats. A few others filtered in, but they stood around with all chairs taken. Angie was about to rush into the staff area, but Enrico touched her on the shoulder. "I'll get more chairs." Muffled voices and stomping feet penetrated the room as Janie smiled at the guests and stood up with her hands leaning against the edge of the chair.

When he returned, he lay out more chairs, and grinning, stood beside Angie. Her face softened towards him while Janie welcomed her guests with a nod and a beam, and then summarised her book. His mind wasn't on Janie and her talk, but on Angie, whose hair glowed.

"Second Chances is about real love that won't go away, no matter how much my protagonists try to hide their feelings from each other. It's about my heroine giving the hero another chance and not keeping her head in the past, but more in the present, and seeing him as who he is now and what he's become. The heroine tries to deny her love, but she realises her life is not the same without him." She took a sip of water. "I have a few passages I'd like to read for you." As she started reading, Angie's eyes flickered towards him and her face reddened. He wondered if Angie felt more than friendship for him or if she was just warm with all the people in the space.

At the end of the readings, Angie rubbed her hands together and stood alongside Janie. She looked out at the guests. "If you'd like to purchase a book, please come next door and then J.D will sign them for you when you present your receipt."

Enrico watched the group huddle and rush through to the door to the bookshop, while Janie picked up her phone and scrolled through it. She looked up as he was about to leave. "Great story. You've got quite a few fans."

Janie sat back down as Enrico approached. "Thanks. It's a great start, but as a new author, it's a chance to get that break."

He nodded. "Of course, but I'm sure these readers will spread the word. Even Angie looked intrigued by it."

She squinted. "Do you read romance?"

He frowned. "Not usually, but I have in the past. I prefer thrillers."

Janie put her phone down on the table. "Angie told me how much she likes the romance plot, mentioning she could relate."

"Hmm." The guests returned and headed over to Janie's table where she started to sign the books. Even Angie came back with a book and got Janie to sign it. Afterwards, some of the guests drank coffee and others drank sparkling strawberry wine.

At the end of the day, Angie and Enrico stayed late to close up. They headed inside the staff room and Angie washed a few of the glasses. She put away the milk inside the small fridge then grabbed an unopened bottle of champagne. "How about a drink to our success today?"

Enrico's eyes widened, not ready for the day to end. "I would love one. Thanks."

She popped open the bottle and poured drinks into two flutes. They sat on the couch beside each other, and he enjoyed the dry, fruity flavour with the bubbles reaching his nose. "What a great day, Angie. Thanks for inviting me."

"Well, you've helped me a lot by making the coffee bar and DJ table, not to mention putting up the banner and welcoming the guests. You're a natural with people."

"I try, but you are too. People flock to you, and I can see how passionate you are about your work. You love books and giving people that escape. I can see how alive you came at this event and how accommodating you are." He put down his glass on the side table. "So what does your future look like, Angie?"

She shrugged. "I am hoping to do better with the bookshop and start having these events next door, but they'll be managed by the company. All they'll pay me for is the space and they'll have to organise the rest in terms of food or entertainment."

"I don't blame you. It's too much to do it all yourself. Having the space will bring in quite a bit of revenue."

"I hope so. I'm looking forward to it." She sipped her drink, her lipstick leaving a mark on the glass. "What about you, Enrico? What is your future about?"

"Hmm. As I mentioned before, I would like to be a detective one day, but not just yet. I'm still finding my feet as a police officer, so I'll keep to the status quo for a while."

"I don't know how you do it, though. Seeing victims and crime, and risking your life day in and day out. You have to be courageous to have this job ."

"It gives me purpose so I don't see it that way. Don't get me wrong. I am aware of the risks and dangers, but I see the good in it too. The rewards outweigh the costs. For instance, seeing the joy on someone's face when their loved one's been found after getting lost, or the laughter in a child when he separates from his parent. Even when I get involved in threats of domestic abuse and can keep people safe. It's troubling to see how the justice system doesn't always work for abuse victims, and how their lives are always put in danger. I wish I could do something more about the system, but it's out of my hands."

Angie leaned forward. "I get that. But you get to save people's lives, too."

"Sure, but I don't like doing that too often. I hate knowing that someone might die on my watch, and thankfully, it hasn't happened."

They drank in a comfortable silence until Enrico stood up. "I'll get going, Angie. Is there anything else you need?"

"No, and thank you for today. I appreciate your help." Angie's eyes bore into his, but he didn't want to misinterpret anything and make any moves just yet, so he nodded and walked to the exit. "Enrico, wait."

He turned back. "What is it?"

"Thanks again for your help today."

He hid his disappointment, hoping she would have mentioned wanting to see him again. "No worries, Angie." He straightened his posture. "Oh, before I forget. I need to varnish the DJ table and get that finished. I'll call you when I'm free."

She nodded. "No worries. Let me know when you are ."

As he walked outside, he couldn't help but notice how much they bonded lately. He hoped it was a new beginning.

Chapter 29

CONNECTION

Angie laughed at a joke Enrico made while she watched him varnish the DJ table with precision in her building space. She had her phone on the coffee bar, playing music from her playlist, and right now the soothing sounds of a ballad played in the background. His hands gripped the brush as it glided with skill across the timber. "I guess without humour you'd go crazy in your work. So how is your work? Any interesting cases?"

He laughed. "I can't tell you about any of my cases. You're a civilian."

"I don't need names. Just general incidences."

He brought her fingers to his lips. "We had a recent case of a man assaulting another man because he stepped on his roses."

"You are kidding?" Angie laughed. "He really loves his garden."

"And another waste of time when a woman made a complaint against a young girl playing her piano at night. So many wasted resources when we should be focusing more on real cases like domestic violence, burglary, and murder."

Angie nodded. "I guess that's why you have many different specialties in the police force. No case is a waste of time if you're somehow serving the community."

"I suppose you're right, but sometimes the more serious cases burn you out, and you need those silly ones to keep the balance and tip the scales."

She nodded. "That is a good way of looking at it."

He eased forward. "I'd like to say you've done well for yourself, Angie. You're a businesswoman, earned yourself a business degree, you're helping out with our reunion in your spare time, and you have your own place. You made it on your own and you should be proud of your achievements."

Her face turned red. "Thanks, but my family has helped and I had the support of my friends. I didn't do it all on my own. You've done well for yourself, too."

His eyes roamed his room "Sure. Still living with my mum, who can be a pain at times, and I don't have much privacy. I guess I stick around to help out my family since my dad died, and for now, it works. My family needs me. But I'll be moving out soon. I'm beginning to feel stifled by my mother. She's Italian, you know?"

She chuckled. "What mother isn't protective?"

Enrico put the brush into a bucket full of water then wiped his hands on a dirty rug over a large tarp to protect the floor. "I smell like varnish now."

Another slow ballad came on. "Oh, I love this song."

Enrico's eyes bore into hers. "Would you like to dance?"

Angie hesitated and averted her eyes, her heart beating rapidly at the way he made her feel. She didn't want to give him the wrong idea as they couldn't be more than friends. But she remembered his sweet kiss and how she regretted it, knowing she needed to protect her heart. He might have changed but he could still hurt her.

"It's just a dance, Angie. Nothing more."

He was right. It was just a dance, so one dance couldn't hurt, could it? "Okay." He grabbed her hand, and she ignored the lightning bolt in her back.

She followed him to the centre of the room, and his arms wrapped tenderly around her waist as they slow-danced to the song. Gazing into her eyes, Enrico brushed his hand gently across her cheek. They swayed to the music and Angie got swept into the romance of it all; his caresses warmed her heart and his breath heated her neck. She became oblivious to the world around her, and in that moment, only Enrico existed. Her focus was on his beautiful, expressive eyes, his full lips, and his strong hands. Angie rested her chin against his shoulder as they continued to slow dance, the silence between them soothing. His arms around her waist made her feel safe, and she yearned for more than his touch.

He ran his fingers through the strands of her hair while his other hand caressed the small of her back. "I can't stop thinking about you, Angie."

Angie could no longer deny her feelings. "Me too." She wanted him to kiss her, and as if reading her mind, he kissed her softly on the lips.

They remained quiet for a few moments, a breath away from each other, as the song ended, and the sounds of the bass in the music provided a comforting background. Then, Enrico dove in, kissing her with more hunger this time. Angie's body melted into his. She moaned as his tongue tantalised her, and his teeth tenderly nibbled her bottom lip, igniting a fire in her core. His mouth moved down to her neck, and his fingers caressed the pulse at her throat.

He pulled away. "You're amazing, Angie."

Angie grinned. "You're not so bad yourself." She cleared her throat as reality settled in. She took a step away from him. "Maybe we should clear things up here."

He gave her a cheeky grin. "You're right. But you do things to me, Angie. I would like to see where things can go between us."

Her heart was beating rapid-fire in her chest, screaming at her to leap. Angie never felt this way before about anyone. Pushing her fears aside, Angie leaped. "Okay, Enrico, let's see where things go."

Chapter 30

AN ACT OF LOVE

Over the next two weeks, Enrico and Angie spent time going out to dinner, pubs, ice-skating, and visiting the city parks. The third week, on a Saturday night, Enrico walked Angie to her door after a movie and dinner. His heart raced as he watched her fumble with the house key, dropping it twice. "Are you okay?"

She nodded. "I have slippery fingers." She eased the door open. "Would you like a coffee?"

Enrico nodded. "I'd love one." As he sat on the sofa, resting his hands underneath his legs, he appreciated the way she glided across the kitchen floor with an air of quiet confidence. She wore a tight-fitted black cotton dress falling down to her knees and showing her sexy, bronzed legs that left him on the edge of control all evening. He liked the way her body moved as she reached up for the sugar, and how her dress inched up her legs as she threw the tea bag into the bin. "So where's Jimmy tonight?" he asked.

"He's out with a female friend who I believe he's getting close to. I don't know when he'll be home."

Angie brought his coffee and her tea on a tray and set it on the coffee table. She seized her mug and sipped but held on to it instead of setting it back down. "I enjoyed the movie. What did you think?"

Enrico took a sip then put down his coffee. "It had a good storyline, and like I said, I love thrillers, but the chase between the stalker and main actress was far-fetched. He couldn't have reached her so quickly at the distance he was."

Angie nodded. "I agree, but movies tend to be embellished for the drama."

In the wave of silence, Enrico noticed Angie crossing and uncrossing her legs. If only he knew what she was thinking right now. Did she want him as much as he wanted her?

Angie continued to stay quiet as she gripped the mug and took another sip of her tea. The way her lips moved on the edge of the mug, and the lipstick stain on it made him jealous of the mug. Her hair flowed gently around her face as her eyes stared at the door, probably expecting Jimmy to return. Was she waiting for him to arrive so she could make her excuses, or did she not want to be interrupted by his arrival?

Enrico moved closer towards her and took hold of her hand. He brought it to his lips, then feathered it across his face. The intimate act made him reach for the hair strands in front of her eyes as she turned to stare at him, her eyes lighting up at the gesture. He inched himself forward and kissed her lips tenderly. She reciprocated by pushing her tongue gently into his own and moaning. Her moan undid him.

Enrico wrapped his arms around her, deepening their kiss. He caught himself as his fingers trailed down her breast. He pulled away from her. "Oh, God, Angie. I cannot stop thinking about you day and night. These last couple of weeks have been so hard whenever I have to leave you. I hate saying goodbye to you, knowing I won't see you again for another few days or another week. It's torment. I dream about you practically every night. You're the first person I think about when I wake up and the last person I think about when I go to sleep. I care about you so much, it hurts."

She smiled and reached for his arm. The door rattled, and in came Jimmy with a look of surprise. He shifted uncomfortably where he stood. "Hey Enrico. Angie. What are you up to?"

Enrico took a breath, not knowing what her brother's reaction would be to him being here. "Hi Jimmy. We just got back from the movies and a meal."

Angie blushed. "How was your night?"

He waved his hands. "Good. I'm seeing her again tomorrow night, and oh…She is my perfect woman." Angie gave him a stern look as if they had a secret language. "Anyway, I'm off to bed. See you, Enrico."

"Goodnight, Jimmy." Enrico stood awkwardly. "I guess I should leave if…"

Angie's eyes dimmed. "If it's what you want." She averted her gaze.

Enrico caressed her chin. "It's not what I want, but with Jimmy here, it might be awkward for you."

Angie shrugged. "We can have a cold drink. He falls asleep within minutes, and he is a very deep sleeper."

Enrico suppressed a groan, as even a few minutes wait seemed too long. He managed a nod. "Sure. I'll have a beer if you have it."

She got up and handed him a bottle of beer while she poured herself an iced tea. The cold of the beer barely quelled his desire. They decided to put on a TV show and when it finished, Enrico got up.

Angie stood up alongside him and he wrapped his arms around her. "Thanks for tonight, Enrico. I had a great time."

"Me too." He stroked her face, his hand lingering across her cheek and brushing over her lip. "Would you like me to go, Angie?" he whispered. She shook her head and led him to her bedroom. He shut the door behind them. Her bedroom featured a double bed with the blinds drawn and modern furniture. It had a cosy feel to it, with a small beanbag by the window.

Angie approached the bed and pulled back the covers. Enrico moved towards her and lifted the dress over her head. Underneath, she wore black lace underwear and a black satin bra. His manhood livened up. She feathered his throat with kisses, and the small act released the floodgates of his passion.

Enrico lifted her and lay her on the bed, trailing kisses around her neck and down to her the edge of her cleavage. His fingers played with the soft strands of her hair falling about her which was so glossy and soft. He dared to gaze into her eyes, wanting her so much. In her eyes, he saw his desire mirrored. She wrapped her arms around him and scraped her nails along the small of his back through his shirt. His breath hitched at the tingle crawling up his spine. Against his neck, she trailed kisses.

"You feel amazing, Angie. I want you so much." His mind could no longer come up with words as her sweet breath enticed him. Their mouths met again in ravenous hunger as their bodies melted into each other. He explored her tongue and loved the mixture of her sweet and savoury scent. He couldn't get enough of her, and he was damn sure he'd need to do this every day once he tasted her. He kissed her deeper and they both moaned as his fingers caressed the outline of her bra and pulled down the straps.

His hands found her soft, delicate breasts. He unclipped the bra and threw it over the side of the bed, exposing her erect nipples. He brought his lips over one breast while his fingers massaged the other one.

Angie reached between them for his zipper and tugged, but Enrico stopped her. "I want you to come for me. I need to watch your arousal, so let me excite you first." Her skin flushed.

He moved his mouth down to her abdomen then lifted her body so he could slip off her lacy underwear. The sight of her naked made him short of breath. She was perfect all over and he wanted to give her the world. He wanted to show her how much he needed her, cared for her, desired her. He wanted to pleasure her as if it was more important than life itself.

Enrico probed a finger onto her clitoris and massaged it gently as Angie writhed against him with her eyes closed. "Open your eyes, Angie." She opened them and what he saw was such a heated arousal, he almost came himself. He clamped down his self-control. He needed to hold off. He could do this.

Her mound was wet and swollen, and his attention drew a scream from her as she arched her back. "Oh, Enrico."

His name on her lips had him tearing off his clothes. Enrico pulled down his zipper, took off his pants and shirt, tossing them away, exposing his naked body. He pressed into her welcoming body and thrust gently into her. He buried himself inside her, then they moved in an easy rhythm. His lips planted over hers. He kissed her with hunger and need, and she answered with hungry kisses of her own, their bodies continuing to move in harmony until they both climaxed.

He settled by her side with her nestled against him as they fell asleep.

Chapter 31

TRAFFIC OFFENCE

Enrico drove through the streets with Peter, checking for any signs of trouble. So far, so good. They might be able to have lunch soon. The past couple of weeks had been pure bliss with Angie as he stayed over at her house a few nights a week. They were getting closer, and he was wondering if she felt the same way as he did.

He was jolted from his thoughts when a madman sped through the main road without a thought to pedestrians crossing or traffic lights.

Enrico put on his sirens and sped through the streets of Brunswick. Constable Peter Jonesy's eyes were full of fear, but he sat quietly in the passenger seat.

"It looks like a crazy man's driving. I wonder what's wrong with him," said Peter.

Enrico floored the police vehicle and swore at cars driving slowly. He hated how people disrespected the sirens. This man could do damage, and he wasn't going to let him hurt anyone on his shift. People usually stopped their abhorrent behaviour only when someone got hurt, and he was there to prevent that from happening.

"He won't even stop." He reached the car and motioned for the driver to pull over, but rather than stop, the driver kept driving in a zigzag fashion, almost running onto the footpath. Again, Enrico gestured for him to pull over but he wouldn't stop. What the hell was wrong with this guy? He might have drugs or alcohol in his system. He kept on his tail.

Peter shook his head. "What's with him, boss? Why isn't he stopping?" He kept his gaze straight ahead with his lips pursed.

Enrico scoffed. "I don't know, but if he doesn't, he's going to hit something or someone." He kept on his tail.

The driver continued changing lanes and suddenly stopped at a traffic light. He continued when the light changed and appeared to slow down until he steered in a different direction. There was a tree close to the kerb and he rammed straight into it. *Damn!*

Enrico and Peter got out of the car to examine the scene. The car was a complete write-off. He peeked inside the driver's side and noticed his head back against the headrest with blood splattered over his face and bruising around the eyes. The face, he recognised.

The driver was his old friend, Jake.

Opening the driver's door, Enrico checked his pulse. He was unconscious but breathing. He got back in his car and called for help on his police radio. "There's been a car accident." He recited his location. "The driver appears to have minor injuries, and I need an ambulance at this location right away."

Enrico turned to Peter. "I want you to interview witnesses and find out what happened while we wait. I'll get drivers to detour from the scene."

Twenty minutes later, the ambulance and fire brigade arrived. One of the paramedics, a short and stout man, walked up to the car. "So what happened here?" The other male paramedic who was of average build glanced inside.

Enrico approached. "He was speeding, approximately eighty kilometres per hour, running lanes, and driving like he was drunk. He slowed down but hit the tree and appears to have minor injuries."

The two male paramedics put a neck brace on Jake, slowly lifting him out of the car and laying him down on a stretcher while passersby and drivers looked on. The paramedics took him into the waiting ambulance and drove to the nearest hospital.

Once Enrico and Peter got back to the station, they wrote up the incident and further worked the case by investigating Jake's background. He peered over Peter at the computer screen with his head tilted.

"Okay, so the man's name is Jake Timmens. Years ago, he lost his licence for drunk-driving and reckless endangerment. He hasn't yet learned his lesson," said Peter.

He nodded. "I know the guy, Peter. He and I attended the same school. Looks like he hasn't changed much. He was a bully then, and it looks as if he keeps putting people in harm's way."

"Right," said Peter. "What do you want to do about this?"

He lifted up his chest. "It's fine. I can deal with this then it's up to the court."

"Peter, can you notify his mother about the accident? One of them will have to contact their insurer, too."

"Sure, boss." He made his way forward but turned back. "Were you and Jake friends?"

"You could say that, but I was as bad as he was back in the day."

Peter sighed heavily. "I know you must feel something even if he was a jerk. Are you okay?"

Enrico nodded, not wanting to waste his time talking about a man he had no regard for. "I am fine. Now, how about we get back to work?"

Chapter 32

HOSPITAL VISIT

Enrico stood at Jake's bedside in the hospital ward after another officer attended to his case. Peter sat in a chair, watching the exchange.

Jake swallowed and picked at his skin. "What the hell are you doing here, Enrico?"

"Why you were driving so recklessly, Jake?" asked Enrico.

"I wasn't well so I accidentally hit the tree. I don't remember anything else."

He shifted his weight. "Jake, I don't know what your problem is, but we found traces of alcohol in your system. You read 0.06 this time, higher than your last incident, according to a report. You're looking at a licence cancellation of six months, and you'll need to attend court to have it reinstated. I advise you to seek out a lawyer."

He shrugged. "I only had a few drinks so how can that be?"

Peter intervened. "Sir, you were cutting off other drivers, driving recklessly, and speeding. Not to mention evading police. You hit the tree because of the alcohol in your system. So this is pretty serious."

Jake peered at the officers, turning red. "But I didn't drink much and I have it under control. I wasn't feeling well." He averted his eyes.

"I haven't been getting much sleep lately and you can't arrest me for that." Jake clenched his fists. "And I don't need a lawyer as I won't let this happen again."

Enrico looked at Peter, his eyes darkening. He turned back around. "Jake, you're going to need an interlock device once you have your licence reinstated. I would suggest you get treatment, too. You might not be so lucky next time if we allow there to be one."

Jake shook his head. "Like I said, it's all well-managed and under control. I don't need treatment."

Enrico empathised with Jake's family, who would also be facing challenges over the next six months. "Jake, we've spoken to your mother and gave her the resources for rehabilitation. At least consider it." He moved back. "Your mother is on her way. And please learn from this, as you might not be lucky the next time around."

Enrico turned to walk outside of the ward with Peter and hoped Jake wouldn't show his face around Angie again. She didn't need a reminder.

"Wait up," said Jake.

He turned to Peter. "Wait outside. I'll be there in a minute. "I heard on the grapevine from Gina that you're seeing Angie. Is that true?"

Enrico glowered. "That's none of your business, Jake. I would suggest you think about your own life before you focus on me." He made a turn, but Jake's voice rambled on.

"How can Angie go out with a bully? That's like a victim going out with her rapist. It's crazy shit, and I for one, think you're just seeing her out of a sense of obligation. You are just seeing her to make yourself feel better about what you did to her. This won't last, and she'll wise up soon enough. If you really care about her, you should dump her. Don't you think she deserves a man who has always treated her with respect? Do the poor lady a favour as I know she can do better than you."

He scoffed. "I thought we were friends back in high school, Jake, but you slept with Gina. You hurt me back then, but now I realise you weren't worth my energy."

Jake gave him a mocking smile. "Gina needed a real man and I gave her what she wanted. Even Angie is too good for you. Have a nice day, Officer."

Enrico rushed out of the ward with his head hung low. *Christ! Jake had some nerve.*

Chapter 33

SEED OF DOUBT

Enrico arrived home and threw himself on the sofa, feeling deflated. He clenched his fists and took a deep breath. What if Jake had a point? What if he wasn't worthy of Angie, given what he had done to her? He had literally humiliated her for years in high school. Granted, it hadn't been every day, but it had been often enough to leave a huge scar. How had he not realised that what he was doing was wrong? Worse, how could someone like Jake see it before he did?

Stella waltzed into the room, energised as usual. "Hey, bro. You look like shit. What gives?"

He fixed his gaze on Stella, loathing her cheerful mood. She must've had a better day than he did. "I had a hard day today and worked a long shift. Some days are so bad. I wished I didn't have to mix my past with my present."

She sat down beside him, holding her phone. "What?"

"Never mind."

Stella sat down and pulled her legs up onto the sofa. She put a blanket over her lap. "Hmm. Would this happen to have anything to do with Angie? Your love interest?"

He nodded. "Yes, but I'd rather not talk about it."

"Come on, Enrico. I know something happened today. What is it?"

He needed to talk to someone about this, and she happened to be available. "Do you remember Jake from high school?"

Stella scoffed. "That creep. What about him?" Enrico explained today's incident. "Christ! And he said all that to you? He has no right, given the type of guy he is. If you listen to one thing he says, you've got rocks in your head, bro."

Enrico knew she was right, for the most part. But Jake had been right on one point, too. "I don't deserve Angie. She deserves to have someone who didn't shame her for two damn years, Stella." His mind flashed back to Angie's bright eyes and full lips. "I can't stop thinking about her. She's in my dreams, and she's the first mental image I see every morning. But I don't know if I can make her happy."

"You are a great guy, Enrico. Don't go thinking like that." She scrolled through her phone. "Have you been intimate with her?"

He tilted his head. "Good to know you're focused on your phone."

She grunted. "A girl can multi-task, more than men actually. Have you?"

"It's none of your business."

Stella gave him a reassuring smile. "Stop overthinking this and really get to know her, bro. She's worth it. I'm sure."

Enrico grinned "I don't know."

Stella's eyes shifted back onto Enrico. "Take it nice and slow, and don't make any rash decisions."

"I will see you later, sis." He strode to his bedroom and wished he hadn't seen Jake again after all these years. Seeing Jake again reminded him of who he once was, and he hated that guy with a vengeance. He didn't want to think about how he had ruined Angie's life. Enrico wished more than anything he could take it all back. He pushed down his fury at himself, took a breath, and sat on his bed. He retrieved his phone and searched through his contacts. He wanted to click on Angie's number, but his fingers were frozen.

Instead, he picked up his laptop and checked his emails, but his mind wasn't on his messages. It was on Angie, and he missed her. It had only been a few days since they made love and he still craved every inch of her. But would it be fair to her? He had called her last night, and they talked for over an hour. He could never tire of her voice.

His phone buzzed. He picked it up from his bedside table, noticing it was Angie.

"Hi Angie."

"Are you okay, Enrico? You sound a bit flat."

He didn't want to explain seeing Jake again. "Sure. How are you?"

"Great. I wanted to invite you over to my mum's place for lunch on Sunday. Are you free?"

Enrico briefly closed his eyes, not wanting to meet her mother who would surely judge him when he wasn't sure about the relationship. "I don't think I can make it, Angie. Sorry."

"Have you got something else on?"

He took a deep breath, not wanting to lie to her. "No, I'll be home. I'm just...not ready to meet your family." Silence. "Angie? Are you there?"

"I'm here. It's fine if you're not ready, but I can sense something else is going on here. Did something happen between last night and tonight? You sounded great over the phone last night, so what happened?"

"Nothing I wish to get into over the phone, Angie. We should talk face to face."

"Listen, Enrico. Whatever you have to say, just say it. I won't sleep tonight with you sounding the way you do. What's going on?"

"Angie, I...I think we should take a breather here. Maybe we moved a bit too fast. I'm sorry."

She gasped. "By breather, do you mean you're breaking up with me?"

"No, I just think we need a break. I have to think things through, and I've got a lot in my head I need to clear up."

"Right. What brought this on?"

Enrico gripped the phone, the back of his head compressing. "I really can't get into it. Please, Angie. Try to understand, I need some time to get my head around things."

"What things? You're not making sense. You were the one who came after me and now you want to break it off?"

"Just a bit of space, that's all. I will call you soon."

"If you can't explain what this is really about, then don't bother. Bye, Enrico." She ended the call, and the silence at the other end was unnerving. His heart broke in two and he pushed down his tears. He was doing the right thing.

Chapter 34

STILL A BULLY

Inside the shop, Angie reached into a box and pulled out books, setting them down on the front counter. She lifted and released her shoulders, pressing her fingers into the crook of her neck to prevent further aches. Maddy picked up the books from the counter and placed them out front near a display sign stating, *New Book Releases - in hardback and paperback*. Angie emptied the box and stored it underneath the counter.

It had been one week since she last spoke to Enrico, and she wondered if he would ever call her again. That night he had mentioned wanting a breather, but he hadn't explained why. Angie had cried into her pillow and punched it until her knuckles were sore. A deep fury overcame her. What had prompted him to want to have this break? Was it her?

She started to think that he hadn't really changed at all, that he was playing games with her. Was that all she was to him? A game? A challenge to overcome? Now that he had had his way with her, would he spread the word to all his friends, saying how easy she was?

When Angie straightened, she noticed a male customer standing with his back to her. Something about the man looked familiar. He was tall and lanky with short, black waves. He wore skin-tight jeans with a white t-shirt. His black hair looked messy and unwashed. When the man turned, walking towards her with a slight limp, Angie became speechless. Her body froze and her feet stayed glued to the floor.

Jake's dark-brown eyes bore into hers. He had bruising on his face as if he'd been in an accident. She'd say he was definitely a ladies' man, good-looking on the outside but ugly on the inside, if she didn't despise him so much.

"Hi, Angie. Nice place you have here." When Angie didn't respond, he went on. "I'm looking for a specific book." He gave her a sticky note. "Do you have it?" Angie shook her head without viewing the note. "Why are you here, Jake? What do you want?" She stood frozen behind the counter while Maddy tidied up the store and greeted other customers.

"I need this book," he said.

Angie squinted in confusion, but when she glanced at the note, she winced. "You want a book called, *He Only Pities You?* Is that supposed to be a message?" As Angie led him closer to the staff room, away from the browsing customers, her stomach tightened and her fists clenched. What was this man up to?

Jake gazed at her with a mocking smile. "If you didn't get the message, it is to say that Enrico only pities you. He saw you as a challenge, and a way to compensate for his past. I'd say if he banged you, then he's a clear winner." Jake chuckled, his eyes roaming the bookshop. "Nice place. I never thought you'd amount to much, but you sure have done well." He placed an index finger across the side of his lip. "I doubt you could keep Enrico interested long enough. I'm sure he'd soon get bored and focus on someone else. He won't stay faithful to you. He has needs and you will never be able to fulfil them. You'll always be a loser, Angie. A leopard doesn't change its spots."

Angie swallowed and fought back the urge to slam a punch in his eye. "You are the loser, Jake, who only feels better when hurting other people. Now, I would like you to leave my shop. You are not welcome here."

He grimaced. "I will leave. But remember this. He only felt sorry for you, and that's all this is. He is only going out with you because he feels bad for what he did to you all those years ago. He was weak then, and he's trying to compensate for what he did back then. Don't stay with a man because he pities you. Give yourself a chance to find a man who can truly love you for you and not out of guilt or sympathy."

Angie's throat tightened and her mouth dried up. Her body turned numb. Enrico cared about her. He wasn't going out with her because he felt sorry for her. Was he? Angie couldn't listen to this anymore. Was that the reason he wanted a break? Because he didn't truly care for her? No, Jake had to be wrong.

She pushed her way forward. "Please go. I have customers to serve." Without looking at Jake, Angie roamed the store among several browsing customers, putting on a mask of professionalism. She moved on to another customer without hearing the woman's rant about a particular brand of book she was after.

"Bye, Angie. Great to see you after all these years. Good luck. You're definitely going to need it," Jake called as he left.

Angie threw him a glare and fiddled with a display on the counter. This man was the lowest of the low and would never change.

Angie's legs shook beneath the counter and she couldn't breathe. She gripped the counter to steady herself so tightly her knuckles turned white. Would Enrico be one other person who didn't care and would eventually leave her, too? Yet another person who would never love her the way she needed to be loved?

Angie stood frozen like a statue, the shop spinning around her. Masking with a smile, she served customers until the shop emptied. She scurried into the staffroom and lay back against the small sofa, a numbness filling her body. Did Enrico only feel sorry for her? Was Jake right about her being a challenge to overcome? Was it all about guilt and pity?

A tap on her arm brought her out of her reverie. "Angie. What's wrong? What happened?" Maddy took her arm, concern and curiosity in her eyes.

Angie turned to her, not wanting to worry her friend. She had to push down her emotions and get on with her life. Onwards and upwards. She had a business to run and a lifestyle to maintain. "Nothing." She got up from the sofa and feigned a smile. "I needed a break. I'm fine to go now."

Maddy shook her head. "No, you're not. You're not fine. You're the walking dead. I'm going to close the shop early and we can talk."

Angie put up her palm. "No, you're not. It's only another hour. I'll be fine until then. Please, Maddy."

Maddy stood up, her hand still on her arm. "Fine, but only on the condition we go to your place and you tell me everything."

Angie knew Maddy wouldn't let up if she didn't talk about it. She only had a handful of people in her life who would understand her. "Okay. I will tell you everything. Now let's get back to the shop." She squared her shoulders and put on her happy face.

Later that evening, Angie sat on her living room sofa while her friends, Maddy and Gerard sat across from her. She was still ruminating about Jake's words and it sickened her to the core.

Gerard leaned forward, downing a beer then wiping his mouth. "Listen, I know Jake visiting you brought up a lot of stuff, but it sounds like you and Enrico need to talk. It's time, Angie. Get the closure you need and tell the guy how you feel."

Maddy grabbed her hands. "I love you, girl, but I wouldn't be a true friend to you if I didn't tell you that you're miserable without Enrico. You've been pining for him over the last week. He must have a reason for wanting to take a break, but don't believe anything Jake says. He's a loser and will always be one."

"I don't know, Maddy. A lot of things came up. What if it really is pity he feels?"

"That is crazy, Angie," said Maddy. "Talking things out is the way to solve them, and I say you're running scared. I know you know that Enrico cares, but it's the fear he'll hurt you again driving you. There are no guarantees in a relationship, Angie, but you know he has changed. You know he truly cares about you. Call him."

Angie knew Maddy was right. She remembered how he took gentle care of her as they made love, and how he supported her with the author event and her business, or how her chest exploded with desire and yearning for his touch. The way he was able to listen and really understand her, but what if was all done out of pity and to ease his guilt over the past? It was possible. "I'll think about it, Maddy."

Maddy wrapped her arms around her, then Gerard did the same.

Gerard got up. "We will leave you to it, and good luck, Angie. I'll call you tomorrow."

Maddy smiled. "I will see you at the store tomorrow, girl." Angie nodded then waved goodbye as they rushed out the door.

She closed her eyes and lay on the couch, taking a deep breath and placing a hand over her chest. She couldn't get Enrico out of her mind. He was in her dreams and in her daily thoughts, and her heart was empty without him. But she couldn't be with someone who felt sorry for her. It wasn't right for either of them.

Chapter 35

LOST CONFIDENCE

Later that night, Enrico sat on the sofa, watching an action-adventure show. His mind wasn't on the program but on Angie. He yearned to touch her again. He would check in on her tomorrow and they could talk. He was about to go to bed when his phone rang. It was an unknown number, but he answered it anyway. "Hello."

"Is this Enrico?"

"Yes. Who's this?"

"We met a few times before. It's Maddy, Angie's friend. Sorry to call you so late but I wanted to give you an update."

His heart raced and his legs weakened. "Hi Maddy. Is Angie okay?"

"Not really. Look, I don't know what's going on between you two as Angie has kept things a bit quiet, but your ex-buddy, Jake, came by the store yesterday claiming that you pity Angie and have been seeing her as a way to compensate for the past."

He winced. Surely, he hadn't heard right? Why would Jake get involved in their relationship? Was that bastard trying to get revenge?

"What else did he say?" Maddy explained. "I'm sorry. He had no right to say those things. I care about Angie for herself and not because I pity her. He is feeding her lies, Maddy. I hope you believe that."

Maddy sighed. "I am not the one you need to convince, Enrico, and I told Angie you care about her, but she doesn't believe it. As Jake mentioned, she believes you're only seeing her out of guilt and to compensate for the past. You're not, are you?"

He had to fix this. "Of course not." His fingers turned cold. "I will sort this out."

"She told me you wanted a break, and I don't know what that's about, but you need to talk to her. She is downright miserable, Enrico. Make her believe you care about her."

"I will get in touch with her and talk to her, Maddy. Thanks for letting me know."

"You can leave the ball in her court. Make her understand how you feel. Then it's up to her. I tried explaining she needed to talk to you, but I think she is still processing it all. She's really hurting."

His heart broke. He yearned to hold her and reassure Angie he cared. He would kill Jake. "I was planning to ring her tomorrow. I miss her so much." He paused. "Okay. Thanks, Maddy. You're a great friend."

"I'll talk to you soon."

Enrico ended the call. He never realised that Angie had such self-doubt. He adored everything about her. The way she pressed her bottom lip when she was nervous. The way her hair swung loosely around her shoulders and the way her eyes glistened whenever she talked about helping those she loved. What if he had made a mistake with her and ruined their relationship? Was it too late?

Enrico clenched his hands. Sweat formed on the back of his neck as he stood outside Angie's house. He knew he'd be devastated if Angie refused to be with him, but he had to take a chance. He had to let her know the truth. Damn Jake to Hell.

He rang the doorbell, waiting for a few seconds when Angie opened the door. She wore casual tracksuit pants, which hugged her curvaceous body, and a white fitted shirt displaying her femininity. Her eyes were bloodshot with dark circles underneath. She had been crying. His heart dropped into his stomach. He wished someone else had been the one to respond to Jake's reckless driving. Jake should crawl back into whatever hole he had crawled out of.

They stared at one another for a while before he broke the silence. "Hi, Angie."

She opened the door wider. "Hi, come in, Enrico." She led him to a sofa. His eyes took in the cosy ambience of her home, picking up details he missed before. A stack of dishes rested in the sink, magazines and newspapers were strewn over the coffee table, bookmarked novels took up residence on the carpet beside the sofa, and clothes were lumped on the back of a chair.

"Where's your brother?"

Angie crossed her legs on the sofa, and he sat beside her with a comfortable distance between them. They had made love, but now they were disconnected strangers. "Out with his girlfriend. He'll probably be home late."

Enrico nodded. "How have you been?"

Angie shrugged her shoulders. "I've been better." She averted her eyes, fumbling with her clothes as if they felt restrictive. Her body shivered in spite of the warm house. "Would you like a drink?" Her voice was breathy like she just returned from a run and was struggling to catch her breath.

He shook his head. "I'm good. Maybe later." The subsequent silence was unnerving, and he pondered whether to start a deeper conversation. He waited, but she kept her head down as if struggling to speak. He wanted to comfort her but remained still. He watched how she crossed her arms and averted her eyes. He could tell she was bitter and angry towards him, possibly thinking he was still a jerk after what Jake told her. Lies! If he reached out to her, she would most likely shove him away. He knew he had to respect her space for now.

"Why are you here? I thought you needed a break."

Enrico wanted to be honest. "I'm sorry. I wasn't myself when I said I needed a break. I made a mistake. I felt you were worthy of someone better than me after what I did to you in high school." He curled his right fingers around his left hand. "Maddy rang me and mentioned that Jake came by to see you. I am so sorry."

Angie shrugged. "Why are you sorry?" Her hands shook. "You didn't force him to come to my store." Angie knit her brows. "Maddy means well but she worries too much."

"It's fine. You're lucky to have a friend who cares." He gave her a reassuring smile. "But I'd like your version of events and I'll clarify things."

Angie turned away, hesitating for a second before recounting the incident. "He pushed my buttons and made me feel...Never mind." She confronted him. "Do you feel guilty about what you did to me? I know that Jake doesn't as he obviously hasn't changed. I want to know how you feel about the past, Enrico?"

Enrico could wring Jake's neck. "He's trying to get under your skin. Don't let him. Please." He explained how Jake had been speeding and been charged.

Her eyes dulled further. "Good. I hope he never drives again. He could've killed someone."

He made a move towards her, shifting his body but Angie put up her palm. "Please don't. The fact of the matter is I don't know whether you like me for me, or you feel sorry for me, trying to make up for the past. You feel guilty and trying to appease your own conscience. I don't want pity dates."

Enrico's body went rigid. "He got to you. You believe such crap? I told you I care about you. What more can I say to prove I care about you, Angie? I think about you all the time. Can't you see? He is playing you and you're falling for it."

Angie shed a tear. "I don't know if I believe you. Besides, someone else can offer you more than I can. You're trying to make up for the past. I can't deal with more baggage. I just can't. I don't want to be your experiment. I don't want to be used like a lab rat. You're not the man for me. I need to find a man who doesn't pity me. You were the one that cooled it between us, and you might still need to sort out what your real emotions are. You wanted a breather probably because you felt bad using me, didn't you? That's the real reason. Jake may be an ass, but he was right."

His hands tightened into fists and he swallowed hard. "Are you serious right now? I have given you no reason to think I pity you. We connected. We made love and that should mean something to you. I don't sleep with just anyone, Angie. Christ! I can find any woman to sleep with, but that's not me. Don't ever believe I don't care about you because I do. Either you want me, or you don't. Either you want to try to make things better, or you don't. Do not use this as an excuse because you're scared of committing to me."

Angie shifted from the sofa. "I can't be someone you settle for. If Maddy didn't call you, we would've still been on our break, and you would probably have never called me again. You only feel sorry for me because of what Jake did. That's why you're here now."

Enrico was speechless. She was literally driving him away. "No, I was thinking about you last night and how much I miss you." He took a breath. "I planned to call you today. It just so happened that Maddy called me first."

"Right. I don't know whether to believe you anymore, especially when you weren't sure about me a week ago."

"No, I was sure, Angie. It was me I wasn't sure about. I hated how I hurt you. I thought you deserved someone better than me."

"Well, you've got your long break now. Maybe it should be permanent."

His chest squeezed hard. "Are you seriously wanting to break up with me?" He closed his eyes, dreading the response.

"I believe we need a break. I have a lot to consider because I have to be sure about us. I have to be sure that you won't hurt me." She sighed. "You didn't even answer my question about how you feel about the past. That alone tells me a lot."

"I hate myself for it and feel so bad for the jerk I was. That's true, but that doesn't mean I don't care about you, Angie. Please don't do this."

Angie turned away. "Please leave, Enrico. I need time without you."

"Fine. Take the time, but you're wrong about this, Angie." He rose. "Understand this. No-one has ever touched me the way you do, Angie, and I do not pity you." He walked out the door without looking back.

Chapter 36

DISCLOSURE

Enrico sat at the kitchen table that evening, making polite conversation with his mother. His mind was on Angie who wholeheartedly believed he didn't genuinely care about her. She previously expressed a light-hearted attitude, but now he could see a lingering sadness and uncertainty. She no longer believed in their relationship.

He stared down at his hands, his shoulders drooping as he fought against the effects of a bad night's sleep. He refused to live without her, but for now, he'd give her time.

Stella forked the lamb roast, her eyes flicking between Enrico and his mother. She put down her fork. "What is going on here? A corpse would make better conversation than you, Enrico."

His mother lifted her head. "Something is wrong. What is it? Bad day?"

Enrico grunted. He pressed his lips together and took a sip of water, calming down his breathing. "Angie broke up with me yesterday."

His mother nodded. "I am sorry, Enrico. What happened?" He remained silent unable to find the words. "I believe she cared for you after the way you spoke about her. Don't give up on her, son."

He sat back in his chair, fighting waves of sadness. He explained her belief in him pitying her and Jake showing up. "I refuse to stop fighting for Angie. She's going through a hard time at the moment, and I will respect her space. But I'm not giving up on her, and somehow, I need to prove that I care about her."

His mother reached for his hand. "I am sorry, Enrico. Given the past, she might have to work things out in her head. You cannot pressure her. She needs to come to believe in the relationship on her own. As long as you've explained you care about her, she will come to understand."

Stella intervened. "I'm sorry, bro." She faced her mother. "Angie is such an amazing person and if Jake put that in her head, then it means she's still not over the past. It will take some time, but she'll get there. Just prove you care about her. You might need to show her. But for now, respecting her space is a good idea."

Stella and his mother stared at him. Enrico got up from the table and headed upstairs. He couldn't take the sympathy in their eyes and wanted to put it aside for tonight. He was tired of ruminating about it, but he wasn't done with Angie. Not by a long shot.

Chapter 37

PROTECTIVE SISTER

A ngie flicked through stock receipts and put them aside into an in-tray. She shifted in her seat at the bookshop counter and smiled at customers walking into the store. Maddy ran around like a headless chicken, searching for a range of books for an irate customer.

She closed her eyes, remembering the way Enrico made love to her. The way he held her tight and tasted her lips. She loved his huge heart, which was a problem if all he saw in her was someone he needed to rescue. She had to be more than that for him.

Jolted into the present, she grinned at a customer who was holding a hefty amount of books, dumping them on the counter. The books were about fitness, yoga, and interior design. Angie served the young woman who appeared familiar. Angie focused on the woman with the shoulder-length brown-black hair and bright blue eyes.

"Hi, Angie. I'm sure you remember me from school. I'm Stella, Enrico's sister. I wanted to catch up."

Scanning each book one at a time, she forced a smile. "Hi, Stella. This is a surprise."

"I hope you don't mind me dropping in like this, but I thought we could have a chat. Enrico doesn't know I'm here."

Angie put the four books into a cloth bag and passed it over. She leaned over the counter. "It's eighty dollars but I'll give it to you for sixty-five."

Stella's eyes widened. "Thanks. Credit please." After the charge, Stella retrieved and put away her card, smiling at the several people waiting in line. "Sorry, I know you're busy, but I'll be quick. Can we go for a quick coffee across the road as soon as you're free?"

Angie took a breath, not expecting an invite. "What's this about, Stella? I already told Enrico that we don't work."

Stella was relentless. "Just hear me out. Please."

Angie got sucked in by her sweet, puppy-dog eyes, taking a liking to his sister. She owed it to her to hear her out. "Alright. Give me ten minutes and I'll meet you outside."

"Great. I'll see you then." She wandered towards the exit while Angie finished serving the remainder of her customers. It had been two weeks since she'd seen Enrico as they'd been having less frequent reunion committee meetings. She missed him. Every night since their breakup, she hadn't slept much at all. The sleep deprivation left Angie walking around like a zombie.

Maddy approached her at the counter during a quiet period with few shoppers browsing the store. "Oh, honestly. The woman was unbelievable. She made me run around for books on every subject under the sun. In the end, nothing was right, and she left without buying anything. It's the third time she has come in since we opened, and next time, I plan to tell her I'm busy and she's free to browse."

Angie laughed. "Be more assertive, girl. You're too sweet for your own good. Next time, be forceful and tell her she has to make a decision and buy something."

Maddy nodded. "I know. You're right." She turned at a familiar figure walking inside the store. Gerard made a beeline towards Maddy and Angie. He hugged them both.

"Are you okay? You look sad," he asked Angie. She remained silent, uneasy about meeting Stella.

"She broke up with Enrico," Maddy said as she wiped the dust on the counter with a cloth.

Gerard took hold of her hand. "Tell Uncle Gerard everything. What's going on?" Angie explained the situation with Enrico's commitment. "The way you've spoken about him proves he's committed. I think it's you running scared of finding something that could actually work."

Maddy gave Gerard a strange look. "I think the situation with Jake is reminding her of all that she suffered at school. Or is this about something else? Did he resort to his old ways and hurt you somehow?"

Angie shook her head. "No, nothing like that."

Gerard wrapped his arm around her waist. "I hate what that creep, Jake did to you." He stroked her cheek. "Process things but talk to him about it. Start breaking down that wall and learn to trust him. You can only do that when you're open about what you feel. I have seen the way he looks at you, and boy do I know that the guy doesn't pity you. I could see how much he cares about you, Angie. I think you are just running scared, that's all. Scared he'll hurt you all over again."

Maddy clasped her hands. "Why don't you call the guy? You've been miserable without him."

Gerard gave her a reassuring smile. "Yes, Maddy's right. Give Enrico a chance. You stopped it before you gave it a proper chance, woman. So call him."

Angie pressed down the fold in her top. "I'll think about it." She almost forgot about Stella. "Maddy, I have to go out for a little while. I'm meeting Enrico's sister for a coffee. Do you mind?"

Maddy frowned. "Ooh, that's interesting. Go right ahead."

Gerard waved her off. "Go. I'm sure she's here on behalf of her brother, but we'll go out again soon, okay?"

"Sure, Gerard." She fixed her gaze on both her friends. "I love you guys. Bye."

Angie headed to the exit of the store and smiled at Stella who sat on a bench, her eyes glued to her phone. "Are you ready, Stella?"

"Sure. Let's go."

Chapter 38

CLOSED HEART

A ngie stirred her cafe latte, and Stella did the same with her cappuccino while the onlookers in the cafe swarmed in and out like flies. It was a noisy cafe on the main road, bustling with waiters all willing to get customers in and out quickly. The aromas of fresh coffee beans, cinnamon, nutmeg, and allspice brought Angie home to a place of warmth and love. She remembered her mother making cinnamon rolls and showing Angie how to add the right ingredients for the right consistency. It had been one of her mother's happier, sober days.

"So, the reason I wanted to meet was to talk to you about Enrico, of course. He's miserable without you. He broods and whines about everything. Even when my mother gives me the silent treatment, it's better than his miserable self. He misses you, Angie."

Angie's heart warmed. "It's complicated, Stella."

Stella fixed her eyes solidly on Angie's as if attempting to read her emotions. "Tell me you don't have feelings for my brother, and I'll leave right now."

Angie wanted to tell her just that but couldn't. "So he really doesn't know you're here?"

Stella shook her head. "No way. He'd have my head in a grinder if he knew. He's way too proud to share much of his emotions, which is why he probably hasn't told you how he feels about you. Am I right?"

Angie nodded. "He mentioned he cares about me, but I think he pities me more than anything. He's trying to make up for the past, and he no longer needs to do that." She swallowed. "I'm not ready to see him again."

Stella took a sip of her cappuccino then put it down gently. "He definitely doesn't pity you. He can see how strong you are, believe me." She leaned back. "All I'm asking is for you to give him a chance. See where the relationship goes. He hasn't had much luck with his ex-girlfriends. He's a work in progress, but I can tell he's different with you. He's shown it."

Angie rubbed her chin. "Shown it, how?"

Stella chuckled. "Okay. He's been watching a hell of a lot of love stories, listens to love songs and ballads, and his mind is not on his duties at home. He even put the milk in the pantry one day, and I'm sure you were on his mind. I believe he's falling hard for you."

"I appreciate you vouching for your brother, but I've got some things to work out in my head. For now, it's best this way."

"I hear you, but for the first time in a long time, Enrico's happy. I know you're missing out on an opportunity by letting fear guide you. He explained the stories from school, and he was a first-class bully, but he realised his mistake and is sorry. He has a heart of gold."

Angie shifted the topic of conversation. "So tell me about yourself. Do you have a boyfriend?"

Stella's eyes lit up. "I have a boyfriend named Steve, and we do plan to get married one day, but I'm still studying so we have time."

Angie nodded. "That's good."

Stella pursed her lips together. "Steve and I have decided to save for a wedding, but I cannot wait for a life with him. He's in a high-paying job so we'll be okay financially until I can graduate and find work."

Angie had an instant connection with Stella. A woman who knew how to live and be happy with the simple things in life. "Sounds like a great plan, Stella."

"I hope you decide that Enrico's worth fighting for. My mum would really like you, and I hope she gets to see you again after all these years." She fixed a firm gaze on Angie. "I do hope you and Enrico can work things out."

Angie swallowed. "I appreciate you vouching for your brother. I'll think about talking to him." Throughout the rest of their lunch, they discussed movies and books and spoke as if they'd known each other for years.

Angie got up. "I've got to run. It was nice talking to you."

Chapter 39

ONLY FRIENDS

A ngie sat inside the pizza restaurant for the final committee meeting before the reunion event. It was two months away, but they managed to organise everything in advance, leaving only minor things to organise closer to the event. A part of her was nauseous at the idea of the reunion. A niggling sense of doom made her tense. She'd at least have Maddy and Jenna at the reunion, as well as a few old friends she still kept in touch with.

Angie stole glances at Enrico as he whispered something to Ray. Gina kept her distance conversing with Tim and Susie, while Jenna gave a slice of pizza to her daughter, Mia.

Gina constantly glared in Angie's direction. The darkness in her eyes was disconcerting.

Jenna sat next to Angie. "I heard about you and Enrico. Are you guys okay?"

Angie's chest constricted. "We're taking a break. Long story."

Jenna cleaned Mia's mouth as she dripped sauce down her chin. "A break can be good. So how is the bookshop doing?"

"Ever since the reunion meetings, sales have improved, and I'm getting my soon-to-be side business with the event space sorted through advertising and promotions. I have a couple of events coming up in the next few months. They're training events."

Jenna smiled. "That sounds great. You could get testimonials after the events. That will bring in more business." She shook her head, staring down at Mia. "What are you doing, Mia? You've made a mess with your pizza." She picked up a napkin and dabbed her mouth and stained t-shirt. She turned back to Angie. "I heard that Enrico's been handy with the equipment for your room. He is skilled, isn't he?"

Angie nodded, ignoring the way his eyes stayed glued to her. Her posture stiffened and she glanced down. "He has helped a lot to get this reunion underway, and I am grateful." She realised how much he had done for her over these past months, with the reunion, the book signing, the wood pieces, the get-togethers, and saving that woman from dying. He had always been a gentleman when they had gone out, filling her with a yearning to be closer to him. Was she overthinking this?

Pushing down her desire, she focused on her food, taking a bite of her remaining pizza which had become cold and soggy.

Angie turned to Tim and Susie. "Are you guys okay with decorating the shop and getting the DJ to set up a bit earlier?"

Susie nodded. "If you give us the key, Angie, we'll set things up."

Angie nodded. "I'll be there early so I will let you in. I'll text you on the day when I arrive at the shop. Thanks, guys." She avoided Enrico's gaze.

Jenna touched her on the shoulder. "I want you to relax, given we're using your place for the venue. It's our turn to give back."

Enrico faced her. "The caterers will deliver the food a bit earlier that night."

"Sure." She turned to the whole group. "I've hired a couple of long tables for the buffet too. It will all get delivered the night before."

After they finished their meals and shared in the payment of the bill, Angie walked alongside Jenna and Mia. She said goodbye to Ray, Susie, and Tim. Enrico hovered close behind Angie. Gina waved goodbye to everyone and left the building. But her skin prickled at knowing Enrico was behind her, the scent of his cologne drawing her towards him.

Jenna gestured towards Angie. "I need to go to the bathroom. Would you mind staying with Mia for a few minutes? I won't be long."

Angie nodded, wondering if she'd done it on purpose. "Of course. Go."

Enrico stood alongside her then bent down low to Mia. "How are you, cutie? Did you enjoy your pizza?"

"I did, Enrico. I had olives and lots of cheese. Yummy!"

He pulled a handkerchief out of his pocket. "Can I clean your chin? You have some of that sauce on it." She nodded. He gently took off the sauce. "There, all done. You are mighty clean now." He angled his head towards Angie with a reassuring grin. She smiled back in spite of herself. "How are you, Angie?"

She shrugged. Words failed her. The way he interacted with Mia was heart-warming. He had a knack with children. He'd make a great father and possessed a heart of gold. But she still had doubts about his feelings towards her.

"I'll give you time, Angie. But this isn't over, not by a long shot. I'm not going anywhere."

Chapter 40

WORK OF LOVE

Enrico hefted a large shovel and pushed it into the ground in readiness for planting an array of vegetables including broccoli, Chinese cabbage, lettuce, eggplant, and endive. He kept digging and intermittently wiping his brow. The heat of the sun made him sweat, and he was dehydrated. He wasn't sleeping well after his breakup with Angie. He ruminated about how he could have made a better choice when she asked him to see her family.

Putting down the shovel, he took the vegetable seeds and pushed them deep into the dirt in well-arranged rows along a timber bedding. Clutching the hose, he watered them and swept alongside the path underneath the pergola. He took his gardening implements back inside the shed and locked the door.

Enrico sat down on the outdoor chair and rested at the timber table underneath the pergola, an image of Angie in his head. It had been too long since seeing her at the reunion dinner meeting, and he missed her. He didn't want to pressure her while she needed to think, but he prayed they'd find their way back again. Today was his day off, and he planned to make Angie a special gift, whether they got back together or not. It was a symbol of how he felt.

"Enrico."

"Hey, Mum."

She brought him a glass of water and settled across from him. Her eyes roamed the garden and she grinned. "Good work. Thanks Enrico. My knees have been playing up lately, so I appreciate it."

"No problem. I love a good workout in the garden before I go back to the gym."

His mother angled her head with curiosity in her eyes. "What's with the gloom and sadness on your face? Angie?"

He sipped his water then set it down. He fixed his eyes gravely on his mother, his feet shuffling underneath the table. "I care about her so much it hurts not to be with her."

"I'm sorry for what you're going through, son. Things will work out. You'll see. From what you've told me about her, she's a strong, resilient woman, and has suffered far too much for a girl her age. Capturing your heart must mean she has good taste in men but give her time to process things."

"I know. You're right. I've started working on a wood carving for Angie." He slid from his seat and stretched his body. "I want the piece to hold meaning. I have to show her exactly as I see her."

"I'm sure you'll make the right choices where she's concerned."

"I'll be in the garage if you need me."

His mother gave him a reassuring smile. Enrico's garage contained a table laden with tomatoes for making sauce, crates of empty bottles, toolboxes, gardening implements lining the shelves, and his weathered workbench for his woodwork creations.

Enrico put on his work gloves and lifted his partial wood carving of a lotus flower. He set it on the bench and used his chip carving knife to cut into the wood. He had started this project weeks ago, first painstakingly tracing a design of a lotus flower. Taking a deep breath, he turned towards a rusty shelf and picked up a detail wood knife. Bending to his knees, he opened a cupboard and reached for a hook-carving knife and a whittling knife. These tools would ensure he captured the detail in the design.

The box sat inside the cupboard along with his tools. He needed to add more to it but wasn't sure how he could decorate it further just yet. Ideas would come to him while he was working, but for now, he kept the box hidden and resumed work on the lotus. Enrico wanted to remind Angie of her amazing qualities and give her a symbol of his love with his woodwork. The lotus was on its way to being ready.

Chapter 41

PREPARATIONS (ONE MONTH LATER)

Angie walked up the stairs towards the back of the bookshop and bent down to place bottles of assorted drinks, including juices, soft drinks, water, and alcohol into eskies which the committee team members shared. The large window brought in the sun's glare as she walked along the space. Wiping a brow with the back of her hand, she watched Enrico as he hefted a crate of a range of alcohol towards the elongated table. She pulled out bottles of whisky and liquors and set them on the table.

Enrico's friend, Mark, entered the room with a tray of food. "Listen, we can do the rest. You guys leave and get changed. We'll have everything ready in the next couple of hours. Now, do you want these trays of food in the other building?"

Angie nodded. "Yes, thanks. You do have a lot of food, but we are having almost two hundred guests so it should all be eaten."

Mark smiled. "We aim to please." He walked off in the opposite direction and watched the bartender they had hired set up drinks at the back of the bookshop.

Enrico fixed his gaze on her. "I'll go check on Tim and Susie with the entertainment and DJ in the other room." He frowned. "You go on home, get changed, and I'll make sure everything's set."

"Are you sure? I can do that if you like."

He shook his head. "Go, but before you leave, I wanted to ask you something, Angie."

She forced herself to ignore his full lips and his taut chest which played havoc with her heart as she yearned to have him hold her again. No, she had a mission to complete, and that was to get through this reunion and push down her feelings so she could get through the night. She needed to. Her business success counted on her having a straight head, and she refused to let the old students bring her down. She could do this. "What is it?"

"Will you be alright tonight?" He inched himself closer and placed a gentle hand on her shoulder. "I worry about you."

She trembled at his touch. The worry was more about pity and compensating for his past actions, she told herself. "I will be fine, Enrico. I'll be too busy worrying about getting everything to come together; the food, the music, the drinks, and making sure everyone is comfortable in the limited space we have."

"Are you kidding me? You have given us plenty of space with the back here and the building next door. I think you're amazing to offer your business as the school event, given...Well, you know."

Angie's eyes roamed the space with its abstract paintings displayed on the wall and the large window with its view of other buildings and city skyline. The walkway was several metres long. "I'm leaving, and I'll be back later." She rushed ahead, down the stairs and out of the building without looking back. Heading close to her car by the kerb, she bumped into Jenna who had been next door. "I will see you later."

She leaned in. "Are you okay? You look a bit flushed. What happened?"

Angie shrugged. "I'm fine. Enrico said he'd make sure everything else was set. I take it you have the tickets and the sign-in book?"

Jenna nodded. "All set. You go on home and make yourself more beautiful. We've got this."

Angie's heart warmed. "Thanks, Jenna. Is there anything else I need to do for tonight?"

"No, just go home, get changed, and I will see you later here with Maddy."

Angie took a breath. "Okay. I'll see you soon." She entered her car and drove off, her mind churning and turning back to Enrico. She couldn't afford distractions and would not fall into the trap of him playing with her emotions. Tonight was important; a way to showcase her business and talk to people about using the building next door as an event space for the future. Surely, nothing would go wrong tonight?

Chapter 42

SCHOOL REUNION

Angie peered through the window of the limousine which Maddy had organised for the two of them. Her hair lifted on the nape of her neck at the thought of going back into her past at the school reunion. She didn't know how she would manage to look at all those students with a clear head when some of them had bullied her. Steeling herself, she gave herself a mantra about being able to accomplish whatever she set her mind to. She needed to view this as another goal as part of her ambition, and she would get through it.

The limousine driver stopped close to Angie's bookshop, and her and Maddy stepped out and walked towards the shopfront. She still had time to make sure everything was set before the guests arrived, trying to put one foot in front of the other. She clutched her chest when she entered the building next door, waving to Jenna who gave her the guest book to sign.

"You look beautiful, Angie. You too, Maddy." She'd worn a simple black, flowing gown with an off-the-shoulder cut and sequins on the side. A short split displayed the back of her legs while the front, low drape of the dress showed a tad of cleavage.

"As do you, Jenna. Is the family coming?" Angie asked.

She shook her head. "No, my husband's meeting me at the end of the reunion, and Mia's staying at my mum's tonight. We'll be making the most of it."

Maddy leaned in and wrapped Jenna in a hug. "It's great to see you after all these years, Jenna. You were always one of the nice ones."

Jenna's eyes lit up. "Thanks, Maddy. So were you."

Jenna whispered in Angie's ear. "I made sure to tell Gina that Jake wasn't invited tonight, and she mentioned telling him."

Angie's nape ached. "I hope he listens and stays away. He was the worst of the lot."

Maddy put her arm around the small of her back. "Forget about the jerk, Angie. We are having fun, girl."

Jenna gave her a reassuring smile. "Exactly right."

Angie touched Jenna on the shoulder. "Are the rest of the committee members here?" She nodded. "We'll go say hi to the others."

Maddy grinned at Jenna "Enjoy your night without your husband."

She thought about how she hadn't seen the decorations that Tim and Susie arranged as they made their way to the building next door with its strobe lights, an elongated set of tables with a view of the glittering skyline, and well-padded black benches set against the wall. She was in awe of a bunch of plants suspended from the ceiling and hanging down doors and walls. There was a table of finger foods with foiled plates featuring sweets, and desserts for later, arranged on another table.

The glossy floorboards gave her a sense of gliding across the room, and a DJ was setting up the music. The DJ table Enrico made seemed to suit his needs. A banner with the sign "School of 2012" hung above the musical equipment and old school photos were displayed on the walls.

Angie grinned at the whole setting. Susie and Tim approached. "You guys did an amazing job with the decorations. It's beautiful."

Susie grinned. "Thanks, Angie. I can say the same about this gorgeous venue you organised. Not to mention the finger food and catering organised by you and Enrico." Angie wondered if Enrico was around somewhere.

Tim, Susie, and Maddy joined in their own conversation when Enrico arrived with Ray and Gina. Her stomach squeezed tight, wondering why he had to come with Gina, but she had no claim on him so why did she care?

Ray came up behind Gina and kissed Angie, Maddy, and Susie on their cheeks. "Hello, ladies. You are both gorgeous tonight. I might have to steal one of you." He shook hands with Tim when Enrico moved with hesitation. He wore a white, fitted crisp shirt that displayed muscle, and dark, grey pleated pants with shiny black leather shoes. He was like a magnet.

He nodded in her direction, unable to take his eyes off her. "Angie. You look beautiful tonight."

Her heart yearned to reach out to him, having missed him these past weeks. "Thanks."

"Susie, you look amazing with that dress." Gina ignored Angie, her eyes roaming. "And I love what you've done to the place. Simply off the charts."

Susie turned to Angie with empathy in her expression. "Thanks, Gina. But this is Angie's venue which has a lot of space and comfort, so she's done well too."

Without acknowledging what Susie said, she waved goodbye and walked off while Ray frowned and shook his head.

Maddy and Angie greeted two of their oldest friends while Enrico stood silently beside Angie. After engaging in small talk, their friends started talking to others coming into the room.

Maddy whispered. "How are you holding up, girl? Are you okay?"

Angie's throat dried up. "So far so good. I'm going to make some good memories, Maddy and let go of the bad ones. All good."

Maddy held her hand, patting it gently as if warming up her skin. She eyed her. "Are you sure you're okay? We can leave anytime you feel uncomfortable if you want. Let me know, and we'll leave early."

"I'm fine, but if you keep putting it in my head, I won't be," Angie said.

Maddy gave her a reassuring grin. "Sorry. Now go speak to Enrico. Sort things out between you two. Maybe tell him how you feel, girl."

Her nerves were high as she stood there with jittery fingers and a racing heart as guests started dribbling in. She made her way to the staffroom as Maddy moved in to greet the guests, and sat alone on the couch with her head bowed.

A warm caress on her shoulder jerked her back to the present. *Enrico!* "Are you okay, Angie?" She nodded, her throat dry and her head weighing her down. "I know it's hard, seeing a few of them, but think of who you are now and all you've achieved. You have given us this amazing venue. You are not that young girl anymore and I'm not that bully. We have both changed, and I want to prove that I truly care for you."

A tear slid down her cheek as she softened towards him, his body close to hers and their legs brushing. "I'm sorry. I just need a minute before I go back in there."

He wiped away her tear and brushed a strand of hair out of her face. "I will be by your side all night, Angie. Trust me on that."

She nodded. "Thanks, Enrico. It is a big night and I can do this. At least Jake's not coming."

"Gina did mention he wasn't coming, so that is a bonus. You've only got a couple of others who were cruel, but you can manage them with me by your side."

Their eyes locked, and a magnetic pull drew her towards him as he inched forward, stroked her cheek and pressed his lips lightly against hers. She couldn't hold back anymore and glided her tongue inside, needing to feel all of him, needing more, wanting more. All these weeks of missing Enrico went into that kiss.

Someone cleared their throat. Angie pulled away from Enrico, her face flushed. "Jenna. Sorry, I'll be right there."

She walked into the room. "I'm sorry to interrupt, but I thought you might want to get something to eat. Most of the guests have arrived and the hot food is coming out."

"Sure." Angie rose and Enrico followed, making their way to the dining room.

Chapter 43

THE INCIDENT

Enrico nibbled on a vol au vent as he watched Angie chew on a fried dumpling. His mind turned to the kiss he had shared with Angie moments earlier. He couldn't get the taste of her lips off his mind, and he wanted more. Needed more. It was crazy for her to think he pitied her when he was this attracted to her.

All of the guests arrived and Angie spoke to most of them, with the exception of two who had been part of his group and bullied Angie. They hadn't been as bad as Jake, but they obviously hadn't grown up. These guys were in the corner of the room whispering and pointing to her. She looked away, staring at the floor. He could pick out the slightest downturn of her lips, a single tremor, then she steeled herself and focused on the DJ stand with its lights and speakers thumping out the music.

Enrico got up. "Excuse me, Angie. I'll be back in a minute." He put his plate down on the table and approached the two guys. One of them was short and stout and the other one was average height with a solid build. He leaned forward, his face close to theirs. "Hey guys."

"Enrico, my man. Good to see you," said Heath who had a slicked back haircut.

The other guy, Sam, clapped him on the back. "Taking care of yourself, I see."

"Well, you know, life as a police officer, gotta stay fit."

Heath whistled. "An officer of the law! Great job for yourself. Sam here is in pest control in Adelaide and I'm an insurance officer there. Haven't been back in a while. It's good to see the old town."

Sam was sneering at something and drew Heath's gaze. "Right piece of work, isn't she? Some things never change. She may have lost a bit of weight and got this fancy bookstore, but it is just dressing on a piglet." Sam sniggered and Heath smirked. "Am I right, Enrico?"

Enrico took a step into Heath's space, their faces an inch apart. His lip curled up in a vicious grow. "Still making fun of Angie behind her back? I suggest you take yourselves into the other room and stay away from her for the rest of the evening. If I catch you sniggering like children at her again or even glancing her way, you'll be out of here so fast and locked in a cell, you'll wish you never saw me. I'm sure I can come up with something to keep you wasting away behind bars for months. Do I make myself clear?" Sam's throat bobbed and he nodded. "Do you hear me, Heath?"

Heath nodded once, and the two of them rushed off into the bookstore. Enrico smirked and watched until they disappeared out of sight. When his gaze found Angie again, she was looking at him with wide eyes and her lips parted slightly. She caught him looking and turned away, her expression becoming neutral again.

Enrico approached her and held out his hand. "Let's dance." He needed to distract her. His arms reached around her waist as he whispered in her ear. "It's going to be fine, Angie. I've got your back." He pulled away and gave her a reassuring smile. She relaxed in his arms. As the song changed, Angie stepped back and opened her mouth as if to speak.

"Sorry to interrupt," Maddy said at their side. "I need to borrow Angie for some pictures. Is that okay?"

A professional photographer circled the room and took photos of different groups. Angie and Enrico posed with their group of friends. He caught sight of Gina fixing her eyes on Angie from across the room. She had her arms across her waist and a smirk on her face. Unease settled in him.

After the photos, Enrico walked back to her. "Are you alright?" he asked.

"I'm fine. At least those jerks you spoke to are in the other room. Thanks for doing that, Enrico."

He caressed her flushed cheeks. "My pleasure." He frowned. "Can we talk after the reunion?"

Angie nodded. "I'd like that, Enrico."

He escorted her to the dance floor once again, another slow song beckoning them. Angie was somewhat woozy and wobbled slightly.

As Enrico held her tight, she looked up at him. He inched closer to her face and pressed his lips tenderly on hers. She didn't pull away but leaned in, melting into him. His tongue explored hers, and he held in a groan of joy and pleasure. He had wanted to kiss her again for months, and the kiss was sweeter than he remembered. He broke the kiss and held her tight around the waist, stroking the back of her neck as they swayed to the ballad. Angie caressed his upper back as she melded her body with his. The smells of flowers and mint permeated his senses, and he couldn't get close enough to her.

An announcement ringing through the speakers interrupted the moment. They both looked up as he rested his arm around her waist.

Jenna took to the stage. "I would like to introduce the speech part of the night, with me starting." She took a breath. "Before I commence, I'd like to honour my friend, Angie, who has taken the time and effort to give us this amazing venue. Let your friends and family know about this bookshop, and in the future, Angie plans to rent out this space for special events. So if you know of anyone looking to hire a room, this place is it. If you know of anyone who loves to read, then tell them about Angie's bookshop. She has achieved so much over the last ten years, and she has a huge heart and a beautiful soul. Thanks, Angie."

Enrico squeezed her hand as she beamed in Jenna's direction. I would also like to thank Tim and Susie for…" Enrico listened to her remaining speech about all those on the committee and how her experience of Year 12 had been. He turned to Angie when she squeezed his hand. He followed her gaze.

Gina headed to the stage. "Year 12 for me was about setting goals and looking ahead to a life of liberation. We had our highs and our lows, our parties and relationships, and sex, then more sex. It was a wild ride for me, but I managed to get my journalism degree because I stayed focused. I believe we have all achieved our dreams over the last ten years. Tonight is about honouring our time at school and to wonder about new possibilities. Thank you."

Enrico breathed a sigh of relief. Maybe she had grown up after all these years.

They sat down and Maddy and Susie joined them, engaging in conversation with Angie. He got up from his chair, desperate for the bathroom. Seeing that she wasn't alone, he headed to the other room where the toilets were located. On his way back, he picked up a bottle of water from the bar table. Loud voices reverberated in the other room. Fear gripped Enrico's heart, hoping he hadn't heard who he thought he heard, and rushed over. Jake wasn't supposed to be here

.Ray and Jenna attempted to push him out the door, but he shoved them and knocked Jenna to the ground.

Jake approached Angie, slurring his words. "Wow, Angie. Looking hot, girl. I should kiss you again." Angie turned the other way, ignoring his mocking smile.

Jake spotted Enrico. "Well, well, well. If it isn't Enrico and Angie. A couple. Wow. Who would've thought the bully and the victim would get together after ten years? Now he only feels sorry for her. I'm sure he still hates her."

Enrico rushed towards him and pushed Jake towards the door. "You creep. I thought you might've changed after all these years, but you're still the same loser you were back then."

Jake gave a mocking smile while Enrico and Ray grabbed him by the arms and pushed him outside. "I deserve to be here. I was a student. Why did Gina tell me not to come? Not fair."

Enrico hid his fury and made a call. "Peter, it's Enrico. I need you and another officer to come here and pick up a drunkard nuisance. Put him in a cell for the night and let him stew."

"We'll be right there, Enrico," said Peter.

He ended the call and looked at Ray. Jake put a hand over his head as if fighting a headache. Enrico pushed him to the ground, his back resting against the building. "You are in a lot of trouble, Jake. Drinking again, being a nuisance. I'd say you need to get help and a whole brain procedure."

"Oh, shut the fuck up, Enrico. I've got a headache."

He shook his head. "You deserve much worse, you low-life idiot."

Ray scoffed. "A lot of us have wised up, Jake, but you're still an idiot, aren't you? Grow up, man."

Enrico's mind turned to Angie. "Listen, do you mind waiting here. I need to check on Angie and make sure she's okay."

Ray nodded. "Of course, mate. I'll wait with this loser. You go."

Enrico rushed back inside but Angie wasn't in the dining room, and neither was Jenna or Maddy. He walked to the staff room and found her resting back against the couch while her friends sat close beside her in silence.

He approached cautiously while Maddy got up and gave him her space. He squeezed her hand. A deep frown etched across his brow. "I'm sorry," he whispered. "He won't bother you again. Are you okay?"

Angie's eyes shed tears as she let go of Enrico's hand and moved slowly away from him as if wanting to make her escape. "I'll be fine. Thanks for your help, Enrico."

He clutched a hand to his chest. "Jake will be in a cell for the night. You don't have to worry, Angie."

She nodded. "I just need a minute, Enrico. Then I'll come back out."

"We'll talk later, Angie," said Enrico.

Angie shook her head. "No, Enrico. We won't. This thing between us won't work."

Her comment was gut-wrenching, but he pushed it aside. Turning to Maddy and Jenna who nodded, he walked away.

Chapter 44

A NEW LEAF

A ngie waved goodbye to Maddy as she locked up the bookshop. She stood in front of the store, debating whether to retrieve her phone out of her bag to call Enrico. Over the last couple of weeks, she had missed him like crazy, having told him she needed time to sort herself out after the reunion. She had a lot to sort out with her past and, given she had had six sessions with her psychologist, she was beginning to process what happened with the bullying and her home life. It was still a work in progress, but a great start to a new beginning. Why did she hesitate to call Enrico? Why were her hands shaking every time she wanted to call over the last few days? On one occasion yesterday, she made the call but instantly hung up. Squaring her shoulders, she made her way to the car and decided to ring him from home. It could wait.

She reached her car and spotted a familiar figure standing with his back pressed against the passenger door. Her breath stopped and she couldn't speak. Enrico stood awkwardly with a serious expression on his face, wearing skin-tight jeans that hugged his body in all the right places over a faded blue t-shirt that ran over his chest like a second skin. "Enrico. What are you doing here?"

Enrico edged closer to her; his eyes fixed on her. "It's been a couple of weeks since we last saw each other, and my life hasn't been the same without you, Angie. Your number came up on my phone yesterday, and I thought that maybe you wanted to talk. Was I right?"

Angie gripped the strap of her bag and took a deep breath. She wanted to explain what was going through her mind, or they would never work. "I have wanted to call for the past few days but each time I tried I froze."

Angie had been overwhelmed by Jake's presence at the reunion.

"What's keeping you stuck, Angie?"

She watched passersby ambling past then moved over to the driver's side. "Can we talk inside my car?" He nodded, then entered the passenger's side while Angie moved inside and rested her hands on the steering wheel. Enrico waited with his eyes looking forward. She sighed. "I got scared. I am scared, Enrico. It's hard for me to be vulnerable, but I know you've been nothing short of amazing towards me. I needed time, and you gave me that. You've always respected me."

"You're kind, smart, giving, and have the biggest heart I know." He rubbed his hands together. "I understand you're scared. I'm scared too, but we can be scared together and take things nice and slow. Are you open to that, Angie?" He lifted up his hand and stroked her cheek while Angie closed her eyes, savouring his gentle touch. She yearned for him day and night, and this separation had been challenging.

Angie nodded, lost for words. "I would like to try, Enrico."

His eyes lit up. "Great! In that case, would you like to have dinner at my house next week?"

"I'd love that, Enrico." Her heart overflowed with something akin to love but she didn't want to get ahead of herself.

"But for now, I want you all to myself. It's been two weeks too long. What do you think?" She nodded without hesitation.

Later that Saturday evening, Angie closed the front door of her home behind her when Enrico captured her face between his palms and scanned her lips. She became breathless with desire and love as she clutched his shoulders and massaged them gently. It had been a while since they spent the night together, and she felt an emptiness in her gut over their time apart.

Closing her eyes to savour his hands trailing the side of her body, she felt his hand tilt her face forward. "Look at me, Angie. I want you to see how much I love you."

Her heart hammered at his words. "I love you too, Enrico. So much."

They moved towards the bedroom and he lay her down on the bed, a finger softly caressing her lower lip while his other hand stroked the sides of her neck. "You are mine and only mine."

She nodded. "I am all yours." An electrical jolt in her body made her forget the outside world as he leaned into her and played with the buttons of her shirt. Slowly, his hands explored her chest and lower abdomen with microscopic precision. His gaze covered her from her eyes and lips down to her bare stomach as he pulled off her shirt and grazed his hand over the outline of her bra. Angie panted with desire and drew a hair strand out of his eye. Unclipping her bra and throwing it to the ground, he licked his lips and massaged down the middle of her chest before kissing her hard on the mouth, his tongue tantalising and exploring her deeply as she arched her back towards him. Oh, God. She wanted him so badly. "Enrico!"

He gave her a cheeky grin. "All in good time, Angie. I need to get to know your body extremely well."

His lips feathered her smooth skin as she brought her hand over his manhood and felt it harden. He looked up at her. "Tell me if you're not comfortable, Angie, and I'll stop." She shook her head, and with a smile he carried on. His lips planted themselves on her belly button while he stroked her breasts, sweeping down to her hips as he removed her skirt. She wriggled out of it, her arousal obvious in the way her heart exploded out of her chest and her inner thighs dampened. With both hands, Enrico removed her black underwear and palmed her clitoris. With a gentle stroke, her body leaned forward with desire. He growled as he licked the inside of her thighs and gently held her buttocks while she snaked her fingers into his hair. His lips made their way to her mound as he probed her with his tongue, making soft circles as she wriggled. She opened herself up to him, writhing as he tantalised her opening. He made love to her with his mouth and there were no words to describe the elation.

"Oh, Enrico." She pushed her body in further towards him, moaning.

He pushed his tongue in further and massaged her mound hard with his tongue, exploring her body. With two fingers, he probed into her and tangled his tongue, as he tantalised her until she cried out in climax.

He smiled and took off his jeans and undergarments. In his pocket was a condom which he put on. Sliding in her wetness, he gently moved in rhythm, his body fitting snugly with hers. Enrico gave a circling motion as he kissed her hard on the lips, delving deeper and deeper into her mouth. His mouth moved down to her throat, his lips moving down to her upper chest and breasts.

"Oh, God, Angie." He dove into her inviting mouth as they made love with their tongues. Her nails dug into his back while their bodies moved as one. They rose together, struggling to catch their breath as they exploded as one. Looking into her eyes, he hungered for her mouth again, then held her quietly for a few moments. "You were amazing."

She blushed. "You too."

"I can't get enough of you, Angie," he murmured as he nuzzled her ear. He held her close as sleepiness settled in, but their desire soon drove them to merge again and again. Each time he pulled away from her, her heart broke until they united once more.

Chapter 45

HEARTFELT PROMISE

A week later, Angie sat at the kitchen table, watching Enrico's mother piling more vegetables onto her plate. The feast on the table comprised of baked, seasoned chicken drumsticks, steamed assorted vegetables, an Italian salad, hot Vienna bread, a variety of Parmigiana cheese, and homemade Italian sausage. She'd need to go on a diet after devouring this food.

Stella lay a hand across her stomach, wincing. "I feel sick."

Enrico dragged his chair closer to Angie. "My Mum is a great cook but always cooks too much."

Stella threw her head back in a chuckle. "What do you think, Angie? I've eaten too much and now I am sick to the stomach. I cannot walk."

She grinned. "Your mother is an amazing cook, Stella." Angie threaded her fingers through her hair, turning to Valentina. "Thank you for the food. It was delicious." She managed a smile, and Valentina blushed.

"Thank you, dear. And again, I want to tell you I am so happy that you and Enrico were able to work things out."

"Thanks, Valentina. I am glad you invited me over. It means a lot to me." Angie's chest warmed as she watched her glowing eyes.

Valentina gave her a reassuring smile. "I'm pleased you make Enrico happy. Now, how about some Tiramisu? I made it this morning."

Angie was about to explode with all this food. "I'm fine. I will have it later."

Enrico intertwined his fingers with hers underneath the table, caressing them gently. "How about we watch some old home videos on the TV? We can have coffee and cake in an hour or so."

Stella nodded. "I've seen them recently but I'll watch them again with Angie."

Angie intervened. "I'll help with the dishes before the video so we can watch it together."

Valentina shook her head. "It's all good. Stella will help. You can start the video without us. Stella and I have seen most of it so you two go ahead. We'll be right there."

"Okay. We'll see you shortly then," said Angie. She followed Enrico into the living room, and he led her to the sofa, where they sat side by side, their bodies brushing and Enrico stroking the palm of her hand.

He caressed her wrist. "You are amazing." He straightened his posture. "The way you have healed yourself and confronted your demons. I admire your resilience, Angie."

"It's behind us now, so let's move forward."

He stroked her face and held her chin, bringing her lips towards him. "I'm glad your perspective has changed, but please talk to me about anything bothering you." Again, their lips met tenderly, tongues flicking in and out with heartfelt desire.

"Ooh, get a room, guys," Stella said.

Angie pulled away quickly, breathing a sigh of relief that Valentina was still in the kitchen. "Is your Mum coming?"

"Yep. She'll be here in a second." Stella turned to her brother. "Play the video."

Angie eyed Enrico, whose eyes lingered as if he wanted to say something. Before he got the chance to speak, his mother appeared and they started the home movie. Angie snuggled into Enrico. She couldn't remember a time where she was happier.

A week later Angie was led into Enrico's garage. Stella and Valentina had left. No doubt to give them alone time. "What is it you need to show me, Enrico?" Over the past four months they had been solid, and her event-space business was thriving. She even increased profits from her bookshop, too. Both businesses worked well together, and with hosting book launches for aspiring and established authors that brought in more money, too.

He beamed from ear to ear. "I have something which symbolises my love, Angie." He reached into a cupboard and picked up a wooden jewellery box. Her breath hitched. A lotus flower had been etched into the wood on a background of green and varying shades of red. "I need to show you how I feel about you." She wanted to tell him how she felt about him, too. "The lotus represents new beginnings, which I hope to have with you." This oak tree symbolises your courage, strength, and resilience, and that has only grown stronger."

"You decorated this jewellery box? It's exquisite, Enrico."

"I did all these designs for you, Angie. This book symbolises knowledge, intelligence, and wisdom, which describe your qualities. And finally, this heart here represents...It symbolises my love for you." Angie shed tears, averting her eyes. He reached out and turned her back. "I love you, Angie. I cannot function without you. I don't want you to ever again underestimate the amazing person you are."

Angie didn't bother wiping away her tears as she inched her face towards him. "Oh, Enrico. I love you too." His lips brushed hers.

Angie fought back tears. "It's beautiful, Enrico. Thank you. But it must've taken you a while to get this done."

He held the small of her back. "It was worth it. You're worth it." He reached for her lips, feathering them with his fingers, then kissed her deeply again. When he drew away, he beamed. "Open the jewellery box," he said.

Angie lifted the lid of the jewellery box. A diamond-encrusted gold ring lay inside the box. Her eyes looked on in wonder.

Enrico held her hand as he took out the ring. "I plan to have you on a permanent basis, Ms Regio. If you'll have me."

Angie's eyebrows rose. "Just what are you saying?"

"I cannot live and breathe without you. You are my world, and you light up my day each time I lay my eyes on you. You're more beautiful each time we meet, and I cannot imagine my life without you, Angie. You are the breath I need in life. Without you, I'd be a man without water and food. I'd be empty, and you have given me so much love and joy." He picked up the ring. "Angie Regio. Will you do me the honour of marrying me?"

Angie's heart soared. "Yes, Enrico. Yes. A thousand yeses."

They shared a lingering kiss as his hand trailed the small of her back, an electricity firing her up. Deepening the kiss, Angie pulled away. "We should stop before this goes any further."

He grinned then moved to the garage door and locked it. "Do you want to stop, Angie?" She shook her head. He pushed her against the wall and kissed her with hunger.

EPILOGUE (ONE YEAR LATER)

Enrico toasted with a plastic glass of wine with Angie beside him on the plane heading to Tuscany, Italy for their honeymoon. His mother suggested Italy, and she organised the trip with the help of Angie's parents. He shifted his body forward and kissed her tenderly on the lips. "To us and our six-week honeymoon around Italy." He eyed the woman who was now his wife, his body responding to her inner and outer beauty. She got more beautiful each time he saw her, and he was more in love with her each day.

"I cannot believe we're going to Italy," Angie said. "I am dying to see the sunflower field in Grosseto, the Tuscan landscape near Siena, and the famous museums. Not to mention the famous vineyards. We can try Chianti and the white wine made from the Vernaccia grape. I can see it now, languishing in the fields and breathing the sultry air, the greenery, and the rolling hills. I am so looking forward to it, Enrico."

"Looks like you've done your research." He caressed her face. "It was nice of our family to organise this, and I am so looking forward to spending every day with you for the next six weeks. I have you all to myself."

Angie had a glint in her eye. "I cannot believe you're my husband, and I can't wait to have you to myself, too." She beamed. "Luckily, Maddy's cousin needed some temporary work. At least she'll get to have six weeks of work experience in the bookshop and be a part of the events work."

He placed her hand against his lips. "I love you so much, Angie Dellucci. And I cannot wait to spend the next sixty-plus years with you."

"I love you too, Enrico Dellucci. So much."

Angie's eyes shone. "By the time we return, you can start your custom-made handcrafts on the side. Jack said he'd give you contacts, and Jimmy's thinking about helping you out as well. He thinks he can do it all. The youth work and the custom woodworking business."

"Remember, I'm still working as a police officer. But if it does well, I might consider a change of career."

"To new beginnings." Angie sipped her wine. "And to living in the moment."

They rested back in their seats and held hands, heading to a bright future.

Reviews are GOLD to authors. If you enjoyed this book, please consider leaving Lucy a review here: http://mybook.to/Secondchances

Check out my other stand-alone romance novel, *A Tuscan Dream* here: https://mybook.to/ATuscanDream

ABOUT THE AUTHOR

Lucy Appadoo is a prolific reader and author of the Friends In Crisis Series. After a childhood spent reading and imagining escapist worlds, Lucy has put her imagination into stories. Her work as a rehabilitation counsellor, and former work as a counsellor in private practice, have led to an interest in writing inspirational stories about authentic, driven women who manage adversity with strength and heart. She writes in the genres of

romantic suspense/thrillers with significant life themes and contemporary romance.

Lucy's interests include researching crime stories and news to inspire her work, watching crime thrillers and suspenseful movies, travel, exercising, reading for entertainment or knowledge, meditation, and spending time with friends and family. She also appreciates her Italian background and culture, which has inspired her to write imaginative stories about her parents' childhoods, leading to The Italian Family Series novels.

Check out Lucy's website and sign up for a FREE suspenseful book here: https://www.lucyappadooauthor.com.au

ALSO BY LUCY APPADOO

Broken Hearts (prequel to Forbidden Hearts):
https://books2read.com/u/mgrnOD

Short Story Thrillers

Evening Interrupted: https://books2read.com/u/3yZDjZ

The Dreamcatcher: https://books2read.com/u/bzaLxn

Red Flags: https://books2read.com/u/bWZ9W1

Collection of Short Story Thrillers:
https://books2read.com/u/bP5vwj

The Italian Family Series - Coming of Age Family Drama/Romance

A New Life: https://books2read.com/u/mqqwZm

The Beauty of Tears: https://books2read.com/u/bpqwk3

Dancing in the Rain: https://books2read.com/u/bOr7LA

A Life By Design: https://books2read.com/u/3J8ene

NON-FICTION

Grief & Loss

Moving Beyond Grief - How To Shift From Grief & Loss to Joy &
Peace: https://books2read.com/u/mVNzDA

Stress Management & Anxiety

Holistic Spiritual and Mental Health - Building Resilience
and Creativity by Conquering Anxiety and Managing Stress:
https://books2read.com/u/47kG8A

Career Guidance

Your Holistic Career Path - Create Career Change, Satisfaction, and
Work/Life Balance: https://books2read.com/u/bzYDz4